SUSPICIOUSLY SWEET

Samantha SoRelle

Balcarres Books LLC

ISBN-13: 978-1-952789-14-4
ISBN-10: 1-952789-14-1

Cover design by: Samantha SoRelle
Printed in the United States of America

CONTENTS

CHAPTER 1

Owen threw the last batch of croissants into the oven and dusted the excess flour off his hands. Last batch for now anyway. He'd need to make up another before the lunchtime rush for croissant sandwiches.

"Like I'll have time for that," he grumbled with a glance over at his mixer. The damn thing had crapped out again this morning, and this time Owen wasn't sure he'd be able to fix it.

He hooked an ankle around a stool and granted himself the luxury of a full sixty seconds to sit down. He'd been up for hours already and once the store opened, he likely wasn't going to get another chance to sit again until closing. And likely not even then, since he'd still have to clean, get everything set for the next day, do a quick inventory, and then it was time to wake up at 4 a.m. and start all over again.

At least, that was if things went well today. If the bakery was as quiet as it'd been the last few weeks, he'd have plenty of time to sit. Sit and think about all those negative numbers in the account books and how they were adding up to him losing his little shop forever. He groaned and got to his feet. Thirty seconds would have to be enough.

A quick look at the back counter told him the bread dough was still rising and the tart crusts needed to cool a little more before he added the filling. He grabbed a set of clean measuring cups, ready to start making up some more pie dough, then sighed and pushed them aside. He went over to the mixer. He needed to get it working before he could bake anything else, but his time working in chop shops taught him more about taking apart things that worked rather than what to do if they didn't.

"Please be a cheap fix." Owen gave the mixer a quick pat before opening up its casing to take another look. The thing was older than he was and up until the last few months had run perfectly. He respected that kind of loyalty. But it wasn't sentimentality that made him keep the damn thing running, it was the fact he couldn't afford to buy a new one. Hell, he could barely afford to keep the lights on *and* pay his one employee.

Speaking of, it must be almost seven. If Yvonne didn't get here soon, Owen would have to serve the first few customers himself.

Owen *hated* serving the first few customers himself.

A glance at the clock showed just a few minutes to the hour, and he still had to fill the cherry tarts and ice the lemon cakes...

With a murmured prayer he abandoned the mixer to start spooning cherry filling into a pastry bag. Maybe they could be the first *no bake* bakery in the city of Grand River. The novelty alone might bring in at least a few customers.

He folded over the top of the pastry bag and focused his attention on piping the filling into the tart shells.

He liked all his creations equally, of course, but secretly, the cherry tarts were his favorite. The cherries seemed so sweet, but they weren't just some soft little cream puff of a dessert; there was a real bite to them, something that made your eyes open wide and your mouth water. And the crust was even better. Strong enough to hold everything together, but gave just right when you sank your teeth into it, melting in your mouth into crumbly, buttery goodness.

But these were for paying customers, not him. Men like Owen O'Neill didn't get the sweet, sharp things they wanted presented to them on a plate. All they got was hard work, long hours, and maybe—just maybe—the hope that someday their hunger would be sated.

He gave himself a shake. Pastries. He was talking about pastries.

He was placing the last whole cherry on top of the last tart, tweaking the stem slightly so it stuck out at just the right jaunty angle, when he heard the bell over the front door ring. Thank God. He scratched his bare arm, leaving a little bit of sticky filling behind. It wasn't that it was usually a problem running the kitchen and running the register at the same time, but he'd only worn a t-shirt today and didn't want to scare off the few customers who did come in.

"Yvonne!" he called out as he picked up the tray of tarts and carried them out to the front. "Get your ass back here quick! The mixer's on the fritz and I—"

He stopped. Just inside the front door, a man in an expensive coat was eyeballing the bakery with interest, his eyes flicking from the long wooden counter to the glass display case to the small tables along the front window with their chairs still stacked on top. He was unwinding a scarf from his neck with quick, fluid movements and turned sharply at the sound of Owen's voice.

Owen just had time to notice dark hair and a darker smile before he caught the guy's eyes and oh.

Oh, damn.

He couldn't make out what color they were at this distance —that's what he got for living fast without dying young—but the man's eyes glittered with humor and intelligence, like he was the only cat in a world full of mice, and he enjoyed toying with his prey before eating them alive. He looked like he was smart, he was a dick, and he knew it.

He was gorgeous.

Alarm sirens immediately went off in Owen's mind. No matter what he might wish, hot, well-dressed men had no business anywhere near him. Besides, maybe it was the long legs encased in perfectly tailored pants, or the hint of gold at his wrist where his watch peeked out from a perfectly pressed shirtsleeve, but there was something about this guy that he instinctively didn't trust.

He frowned at the stranger. "You're not Yvonne."

The man quirked an eyebrow at him. The sirens blared louder.

"And you don't look like a 'Nana O'Neill', but I'm not one to assume," he said, turning toward the front window where the words "Nana's O'Neill's Bakery" could be read in reverse on the glass. Everything about him was neat and precise, from the way he moved to the clothes he wore to the crisp staccato of his voice. The only exception was his hair. It might have started the day as neat as the rest of him, but Owen was delighted by the way the wind had tousled it around the man's head with wild abandon, revealing just a hint of gray at the temples.

Late thirties, Owen figured. Maybe a little older if he'd had as cushy a life as his clothes suggested. About the same age as Owen himself, but Owen knew for a fact he showed every single one of *his* years. Lifting heavy sacks of flour seven days a week kept him in good shape, but every time he forgot to shave for a few days he noticed a little more silver in his stubble than he remembered.

Feeling suddenly shabby in his stained shirt and apron, he raised a hand instinctively to stroke his chin, nearly upsetting the tray of tarts and undoing all his hard work. It hadn't been that long since he'd shaved, had it? What was today anyway? Wednesday? Or was it Thursday? They all ran together.

He set the tray on the counter.

"Nana O'Neill's been dead for years. Now what do you—Fuck." Owen swore as the timer for the croissants went off. Without thinking, he pointed a finger still caked in flour and tart filling at the man. "Stay."

He turned to go into the back, then paused. "And don't steal any goddamn tarts."

Heart pounding, Owen scowled at himself as he walked back into the kitchen. *Smooth, O'Neill. Real smooth.*

CHAPTER 2

Trevor bristled as the burly baker walked out of sight. "Stay"? *"Stay"*? Like Trevor was some kind of dog he could just order around.

Trevor sneered. If the state of the bakery was anything to go by, the man wasn't capable of commanding a mop, never mind Trevor. That'd been clear even from the street.

He mentally checked his notes. Faded awning, patches of graffiti painted over in a color that didn't quite match the rest of the building. Coming inside, any joy that the little bell over the door—charmingly antiquated as it was—might have brought was instantly dashed by one glance at the worn counter, the tarnished finish on the edges of the display case, and the mismatched tables and chairs. If done intentionally, any of those things could've been cool and chic. Hell, there were places on the north end of town that would've paid a decorator thousands of dollars to distress a counter just the perfect amount, or source chairs that didn't match *correctly*. But in this case the overall look was old and outdated, not in a way that screamed "intentional hipster vintage" but more, "put me out of my misery."

Trevor chuckled. Between the decor and the behavior of the assumed owner, his review of this place was going to be *vicious*, even by his standards.

Oh yeah. This was going to be fun.

Shame, too. The baker was, bluntly, straight out of one of Trevor's more X-rated dreams. Light brown hair cropped close to the scalp, thickly muscled chest barely contained behind a gray t-shirt, shoulders you could park a truck on, incongruously plush full lips surrounded by the sort of five o'clock stubble action stars only dreamed of—despite it being only seven in the morning—and the whole package all tied up in a worn apron like a present.

Happy Birthday to me.

And that voice—deep, with a rumbling thunder that made Trevor shiver despite his best efforts. The extensive tattoos twisting down the man's arms hadn't helped either. They added an element of danger and Trevor had always been attracted to trouble. He wanted to know where those tattoos came from and find out *exactly* how far they went. He'd been too busy staring at the man's everything else to take a good look, but something about the incongruity of the implied violence of the tattoos against the sweet frivolity of a bakery turned the designs into something else entirely. Something sublime almost? The juxtaposition of hard and soft creating its own pure form of expression?

Oh, so you're a fucking art critic now too? Give it a rest. It's simple: dangerous guys are hot.

He was dangerous. He was gorgeous. He was everything Trevor wanted. And for the very literal cherry on top, the man had even been carrying a tray full of his favorite desserts.

But then he'd had to open his damn mouth and be an obnoxious asshole like every other head chef—pastry or otherwise—that Trevor had ever met.

Trevor sighed and walked up to the front counter. He leaned his hip against it and swiped a finger along the top beside the tray of admittedly tempting tarts. Clean, at least. That was a pleasant surprise. Just to be safe, he grabbed a paper napkin from the dispenser by the register and wiped his fingers. He could always look up the health inspector's report later. The things that went on in the commercial kitchens in Grand River were frankly shocking.

Part of Trevor's mind enjoyed a quick daydream about the sort of shocking things he could be doing in this particular commercial kitchen, while the rest went back to cataloging details: past posted hours with no cashier, no fixed menu, only a chalkboard with hastily rewritten listings and pricing. No espresso machine from the looks of it either. The dingy little bakery was beyond sad.

"You gonna want a croissant?" yelled a voice from the kitchen.

"Excuse me?" Trevor asked, half actual question, half shock at being yelled at.

"I said, 'You gonna want a croissant?' They just finished, but I ain't carrying a hot pan all the way out there if you don't want one."

"No. Thanks."

A moment later the man reappeared, wiping his hands on a dishtowel that he slung over a broad shoulder. "So, what do you want?"

"You talk to all your customers this way?"

"Naw, only the ones who act like they're too good for this place."

Trevor froze, shocked.

The man smirked. "Yeah, not as dumb as I look. Now what do you want?"

Well, if he was going to be like that about it...

"I don't know," Trevor said as condescendingly as he could. "I have a *very* important meeting later today with some *very* important people who share my *very* high standards. Why don't you just give me a dozen of what you consider your best, and we'll see if that's good enough."

The man glared at Trevor. For a long moment he didn't move. Then, with a tic of his jaw, he turned and grabbed a cardboard box and started filling it. Trevor leaned back to see what the man was grabbing out of the case. To his surprise, rather than grab a dozen of a single item, he was picking and choosing one or two from each of the selections of cakes and pastries on display.

"They're all the best," the man said as he laid a cherry tart carefully into the box. Trevor took a moment to marvel at the skill and delicacy apparent in those large, rough hands, then gave himself a mental shake.

"Best in the goddamn city." The man folded up the lid on the box. "Those croissants you didn't want are the best in the goddamn state."

"I'm sure they are." Trevor scoffed. "What kind of coffee do you have?"

"Black."

"Well then, I'll have a small black coffee too. Please."

The coffee was, he grudgingly allowed, both poured efficiently—and by someone with excellent triceps, not that Trevor noticed—and of excellent quality.

"Total's $26.73."

"Oh, you know what? Throw in a croissant for me too. To go."

Something deep inside Trevor trilled with delight at the baker's flat glare. Yes, this review was going to be a *delight* to write.

The man stomped off and returned with a single croissant in a small paper bag. He rang up Trevor's new total.

"$28.62."

Trevor handed over two crisp twenties. While the man counted out his change, Trevor idly tore a corner off the croissant and popped it in his mouth.

His knees immediately went out from under him and he grabbed the counter as his eyes rolled back in his head. Oh God. Trevor had had pastries personally crafted by Michelin rated pâtissiers that weren't as good as this. Hell, Trevor had had orgasms that weren't as good as this.

The croissant was rich, buttery, but still so light and flaky that it didn't seem possible for something so simple to taste so good. After the satisfying crispness of the outer layer, the rest was so tender it outright dissolved in his mouth, leaving behind a warm feeling of contentment... and a desperate desire for more. The fact the croissant was still hot from the oven only added to the absolute bliss.

His eyes fluttered open, warmth still rippling through him, right before the man looked up from the register and reached out to hand him his change. His fingers brushed Trevor's palm as he passed him his money, and Trevor's knees nearly went weak again. He steeled himself just enough to pocket the bills before dumping the few coins into an empty jar labeled "TIPS".

"For the excellent service," he said, frankly impressed at his own ability to be such an asshole while his body was still reeling from a life-altering experience.

The man clenched his fists and placed them both deliberately on the counter, knuckles down so the joints cracked as he leaned forward. His eyes flashed as he breathed out slowly through his nose, jaw clenched in absolute rage. He had a scar, Trevor could see now, or possibly several. It cut through the tattoos on the man's bicep then disappeared up under his shirtsleeve only to reappear from the collar of his shirt to lick up his neck.

Trevor wanted to lick up his neck. He held his breath as the air crackled between them. His heart beat faster. He should be terrified.

He was *thrilled*.

Just at that moment, the front door burst open, the bell above it chiming wildly. A young woman rushed in, pulling up her long black braids as she went.

"Sorry, Owen!" she said around the hair tie in her mouth. "I know, I know. I didn't mean to be late, but there's bad ice, you should be thankful your commute is what it is."

She stopped when she noticed Trevor, and gave him a quick scan. "Who's this?"

Before Trevor had a chance to respond, she let out a gasp and rounded on the baker, *Owen* apparently. "Tell me you are not making that face at a paying customer!"

She couldn't have come up any higher than Owen's shoulder, and the man could probably bench press at least three of her, but a slight flush colored his cheeks when she put her hands on her hips with an exasperated, "*Really,* Owen?"

It was like watching a Pomeranian dress down a Doberman.

Trevor gave Owen a wink before smoothing his grin into something less venomous and sauntering over to the woman.

"Trevor Hill. Just 'Trevor' though, please. And you must be the lovely Yvonne that our friend Owen here mistook me for when I came in. I'm flattered by the comparison, although it hardly does you justice."

Rather than the giggle or awkward smile he'd been expecting, Yvonne merely gave him a look eerily similar to the one Owen was sporting.

"Are you shitting me?" she said flatly.

Oh, Trevor liked her. Trevor liked her a lot.

With a laugh, he collected his purchases from the counter, pastry box in one hand, coffee in the other. He did have work to be getting to after all. It certainly had nothing to do with a deep voice, broad shoulders, or incongruously warm brown eyes that were still fixed on Trevor so hard he had to suppress a shiver.

She reached out and opened the door for him, then stepped away as Trevor caught it with his foot. He nodded in thanks, barely containing his excitement at the knowledge that he was only a few steps from his car. There he'd be out of sight from watching eyes—warm brown or otherwise—and could enjoy the rest of his divine croissant in peace. He scrunched his nose as the winter sun hit his face, causing him to blink. Just a few more steps to freedom.

"How was it?" that heavy rumble of a voice called out behind him.

Trevor turned. Owen nodded toward the croissant balanced carefully on top of the pastry box, a noticeable chunk missing. "Best in the state?"

"Honestly?" said Trevor as the door swung closed behind him. "It was a little dry."

CHAPTER 3

Dry? Dry! Who the fuck did that fox-faced little asshole think he was anyway, calling Owen's croissants dry?

Owen picked up the mass of bread dough and slammed it down on the counter. In one practiced movement, he folded the dough in half, pressing forward with the heels of his palms, before grabbing the far end of the dough, lifting the whole thing up again, slamming it down, and repeating the process.

If Yvonne hadn't come in just then…

Owen grunted as he threw the dough down again and kneaded it roughly. If Yvonne hadn't come in then, he didn't know what he would've done. He'd been working on his temper. Hell, he'd been working on his temper ever since Nana made it a condition of her taking him in after juvie. When he was seventeen and angry at the world and everyone in it, she'd kept him, even when the rest of his family had turned him away. And all she'd asked in return was the promise he'd keep his stealing to the cookies and his punching to the dough. He hadn't always kept that promise—there were enough years on his adult record to prove it—but every time he'd gotten out of prison she'd taken him back, given him a pinch on the ear, and made him promise to try again.

She'd taught him everything she knew in her cozy kitchen and the only times she'd ever gotten mad at him were when he'd over-whipped the egg whites or gotten locked up again before the holiday baking rush. She was the one he had to thank for his entire business, God rest her hard-drinking, blaspheming, poker-cheating soul.

But that man today—Trevor fucking Hill—made Owen want to break his promise like no one else before. The way he'd leaned all over Owen's counter like he owned the place, long fingers running along the grain of the wood. That look in his eyes—green, Owen now knew—calculating, sizing Owen up. Like he had the kind of smarts that usually sent Owen running, but this time just made him want to snap back instead. That dark, dry sense of humor, and that last shot as he'd sashayed out the door wasn't like a "Fuck you"—more like a "We both know I'd fuck you up, and you'd love it."

Owen threw the bread down again. Or maybe he was just projecting.

It wasn't exactly easy to keep an active social life when you were up to start baking at four in the morning, seven days a week. Not to mention the fourteen-to-sixteen hour days, the paperwork, the orders from suppliers who'd try to nickel-and-dime you for every goddamn thing. Living in the tiny apartment above the bakery didn't exactly help his prospects either.

If there was a bar Owen could pass on his way home—a place to pick up some company, even just for a night—that'd be something. Maybe one with a dark alley out the back or a short cab ride to a stranger's place. Just a quick, meaningless release of tension. God, that would be nice. It'd been way too damn long.

He startled as the mixer let out a whine and kicked up on its own for a few turns before rattling to a stop with a grind of metal on metal. Owen smiled. *You and me both, buddy.*

Still, even if his apartment was too run-down for Owen to bring even the easiest one night stand back to, he was lucky the bakery had come with it. He didn't regret sinking all his nana's life insurance payout into Nana O'Neill's. He was proud of his bakery and the work he'd put into it, but it would be nice to go home to a place without the lingering smell of powdered sugar for once. Maybe even one with another warm body waiting in bed for a bit of fun before his few hours of sleep. Someone feisty, with enough years on him to know what he was doing. Who wouldn't just let Owen put him in his place but would push back, want to give as good as he got. Now there was a thought.

He scowled as he realized the direction his thoughts were heading and threw the dough down again, hard enough to rattle the metal counter.

"...Owen. Owen. Owen. Owen!" Yvonne stood in the doorway between the kitchen and the storefront. He hadn't noticed her.

"What?" he snarled.

"Whatever you're doing back here, cut it out. You're scaring the customers."

"Both of them?" Owen dropped the dough into a bowl with a clatter and covered it with a damp towel. It needed to rest again before he formed it into loaves anyway.

When he turned back, Yvonne was giving him a long, assessing look.

"What?"

"Are you okay?"

"Sure. How do you feel about sourdough?"

"For yours? I'd beat up a nun." Yvonne looked pointedly at the bowl of regular dough in his hands. "Still got some frustrations to work out?"

Owen just grunted and pushed the bowl into the corner where he wouldn't knock it over.

"He really riled you up, huh?" she asked. He didn't need to ask who she meant.

"It doesn't matter," Owen said, as he walked over to the dry storage to grab another bag of flour. "It's not like he's coming back."

CHAPTER 4

"You have to go back."

"I know." Trevor groaned, sinking into his chair. He'd gotten to his desk, notepad out, ready to sample and dissect each of the pastries, but when he'd taken his first bite of cheese danish he'd immediately picked up the box and carried everything into his editor's office. Partially because Rachel would kill him if he didn't share and partially because he was pretty sure he couldn't stop himself from eating the entire box and needed her to save him from himself.

"No," Rachel said, digging a tooth under a perfectly manicured nail to get out the last bit of glaze. "You really, really have to go back. I'm not saying this as your editor for any sort of journalistic integrity crap. I am saying this as a woman, and also your boss. If you don't bring me more of those double chocolate muffins, you're fired."

"No, I'm not."

"No, you're not. But suitable punishment will be had. Maybe La Mesa Caliente deserves a follow-up review."

"Ugh, *anywhere* but there," Trevor said as he licked a finger and dabbed up the last few flakes of pastry. He covered his mouth too late to catch a self-satisfied burp. As a professional restaurant critic, he usually ate sparingly, having only a few bites of each dish before moving on. He and Rachel had eaten the entire box, down to the last flake of filo and the last crumb of choux. He was pretty sure he couldn't move. He might die. But what a way to go.

At least he didn't really have to be anywhere the rest of the day. Aside from early seatings and the occasional lunch, his job really didn't take up that much of his daylight hours. Sure, he was often up until 4 a.m. working on his restaurant reviews, but his work-life balance was his business. Besides, he didn't think this review would take too long, as long as his thesaurus had enough synonyms for "orgasmic".

"What was it you said about Caliente's gazpacho? That it tasted like a can of SpaghettiOs seasoned by—"

"—a six-year-old with a toothpaste fixation." Trevor grimaced, his overly full stomach roiling at the memory. "And I should know. I went through a mad scientist phase when I was a kid."

"That explains a lot."

It did, actually. Mad science and cooking turned out to be quite similar, at least the way Trevor did them. He'd spent years trying to learn to do one or the other correctly, but finally, as a starving twenty-something with an English degree in one hand and a half-burnt, half-crunchy cup of ramen in the other, he'd decided to embrace the motto: Those who can't do, review.

Rachel popped the top button on her pants and Trevor, always one to know a good idea when he saw it, did the same.

"If we get arrested for public indecency I'm blaming you."

"Don't talk to me. I'm too busy digesting to talk. My God, did you try that honey thing with the blueberries? Look at my arm, I still have goosebumps. Finding this place is the single greatest thing you've ever done for me."

"I've literally saved your life before."

She waved a hand lethargically. "Without those pastries,

what kind of life was it really?"

He grinned, too full of buttery deliciousness to properly respond. He hadn't technically saved her life, just given her the Heimlich maneuver when she'd made the mistake of reading one of his reviews and eating lunch at the same time. When she was in a good mood, she said he saved her life, in a bad mood, she described the same incident as the time he tried to kill her. She was his boss as well as his friend, so he supposed he could forgive her.

Rachel had her head tipped back like a cat's, soaking up the sunlight from the office window. The light glittered through her short red hair, the color reminding him of the cherry tart he'd just devoured along with all the other pastries. God, that tart. It was hands down the best thing he'd eaten since becoming Mr. Tasty.

At first, Trevor always tried to find at least *something* positive to say about each restaurant he reviewed, but La Mesa Caliente had broken him. When he woke the next morning to discover the tirade he'd emailed to the *Grand River Chronicle* had been published on their website and gone viral, he was shocked. When the *Chronicle* and *Bon Appétit* got in a bidding war over the right to publish his next review, he'd had to go lie down.

And like that, "Mr. Tasty's Guide to Taste" had been born.

Within a few years, he was the most popular restaurant critic in the entire city. Well, popular amongst those who read his column, at least. But what were a few death threats from chefs here and there? That was why he had a secret identity after all. As long as no one knew that Mr. Tasty was actually Trevor Hill, mild-mannered journalist, he was fine.

Besides, it turned out that a life of infamy paid well. Very,

very well.

"Don't worry, I'm definitely going back. I have to get those two or three visits in for an 'authentic experience' anyway."

"Damn right you do." Rachel gave a quick flick of her wrist. "Now get out of here. I have interns to yell at and a food baby to digest, neither of which will be pretty."

Trevor chuckled, and tried to push himself up from his chair. Tried.

He groaned. "I'm not sure I can."

CHAPTER 5

Owen pressed the heels of his palms against his forehead, trying to ward off the impending headache. For once, the smell of baking snickerdoodles drifting out of the oven wasn't comforting him at all. His supplier was upping the price on cake flour again. Owen wasn't going to disgrace his nana's cake recipes by using all-purpose flour—she'd rise up out of her grave to smack him with a spoon if he tried—but cutting out cakes would leave him with an empty bottom row on the display case.

A terrifying thought occurred to him. What if he tried to make something new?

He knew his grandmother's recipes by heart, but what if he tried something of his own? He'd been thinking of tweaking that apple pie recipe into some kind of a cobbler instead. Or there was that mini-baklava idea he'd come up with in the shower. After all, he had an in for some locally sourced honey...

Owen hesitated. He'd never tried any of his own recipes before, just the ones that had been handed down by his nana from her nana from her nana all the way back to the Old Country.

He growled and scratched out the last few figures he'd written down with more force than was strictly necessary. He'd scrape by with the cakes somehow. Owen knew what he was good at and stuck with what he knew. Historically, him getting creative tended to end in bloodshed and tears. Literally.

Maybe he could find a new flour supplier. He huffed. Yeah, using all that spare time he had when he wasn't lounging around his penthouse and fighting off hordes of underwear models.

His melancholy was broken by Yvonne's voice from the front. "Owen! You owe me an hour overtime!"

Owen frowned. He and Yvonne didn't have any bets currently running except—

"Oh, *Hell* no."

Owen stood up from his desk/least sugar-covered prep station and stormed to the front counter. There, he saw a familiar form decked out in navy blue this time, some kind of sophisticated cut that Owen would wager all the money he didn't have was designer, with a tan scarf wrapped around his neck. The man turned and winked when he saw Owen.

"You. Out." Owen snarled, pointing at the door.

"Owen!" Yvonne chided.

"Yes, Owen," said Trevor, "that's no way to treat a customer. Especially one here to place another large order."

Owen hesitated, Trevor was the only customer in the store and he could definitely use the sale, but still, a man had his pride. And Trevor just pushed all of his buttons. He made Owen want to shake him or throttle him or find some other way to shut up his smart mouth.

He crossed his arms. "So, all your very important friends didn't think my croissants were too dry then, huh?"

Owen tried to keep the hurt and sting out of his voice, but if the pitying look Yvonne shot him was anything to go by, he did a piss poor job of it.

Trevor's face softened.

"I suppose they were acceptable." He hesitated. "I've been ordered to buy more of those double chocolate muffins…"

"I'll get those for you right away!" Yvonne said with her cheery customer service smile. "And another assorted dozen as well?"

"Please. Different ones from last time if you can."

"Of course!"

Owen watched as Yvonne boxed up a selection of goodies, only putting one or two back when she grabbed something he'd given Trevor last time. Owen was impressed, she knew him too well.

"And a small coffee too, please."

"I'm afraid we don't have anything fancy, just black," she said apologetically. "But we do have cream and sugar."

"I know. That's fine." Trevor looked directly at Owen and smiled that shit-eating grin. "I'll take some sugar if you're offering."

Owen rolled his eyes and walked back into the kitchen. *That smug, stuck up little…*

He turned off the timer just before it went off and pulled the tray of snickerdoodles out of the oven.

"I'm gonna wipe that goddamn look off his goddamn face."

Owen lifted one of the fresh cookies off the pan with a spatula. He slid it onto the plate and walked back to the front counter just as Yvonne handed Trevor his change. "Here," he said, clattering the plate down next to the box with "Nana O'Neill's" stamped on the lid. He leaned in. "Careful, it's *hot*."

A brief flash of surprise crossed Trevor's face before it settled back into haughty indifference.

"Is it a dinner plate served on a smaller plate?"

Owen grit his teeth. Maybe his portion sizes were a little

large, but they were the size Nana had always made for him. Sure, most people didn't have quite the appetite of a teenage Owen O'Neill, but still.

"It's a snickerdoodle. On the house. What do you think?"

Trevor carefully picked up the edge of the cookie, bending it gently until a small piece tore off, then locked eyes with Owen as he slowly put the piece in his mouth, closing his eyes as he chewed. Owen waited impatiently.

"Well?" he finally asked. It didn't take a man that long to decide what he thought about a cookie. "Better than the croissant?"

"It is," Trevor said thoughtfully. He finally opened his eyes and looked at Owen through his lashes. "But I suppose the bar was pretty low to begin with."

Owen growled and stomped back into the kitchen. He grabbed a bag of brown sugar and the butter he'd left out to soften. Even if it killed him, he was going to bake something that asshole would have to admit was delicious.

He didn't notice Trevor slide the rest of his cookie into the box of pastries, or the look of disbelief that Yvonne gave them both.

CHAPTER 6

Trevor managed to stay away an entire week before going back to Nana O'Neill's.

Not by choice, but because Rachel had ordered him to lie low. Apparently, she'd been sent a link to an entire subreddit of angry chefs trying to figure out Mr. Tasty's identity. None of them were even close—Trevor's favorite theory was the cabal of competing chefs one, although Rachel preferred Gordon Ramsay in drag, herself—but they decided that being a slightly less familiar face around the restaurants he was about to hit was probably a good plan.

He should've stayed away from the bakery even longer but, well. There was only so much a man could take. He sometimes had to adjust himself if he thought about that snickerdoodle for too long. Besides, it was Rachel's idea for him to branch out from regular restaurants to reviewing "alternative options" anyway. If she thought Trevor was going to be caught dead in a cupcakery or waiting in line at a gourmet food truck then that was her problem. He hadn't even meant to go into Nana O'Neill's that first time either. He'd just seen it while driving and thought about how funny it would be if his next review was on the most boring, run-of-the-mill bakery he could find, instead of some gourmet delicatessen. And look how that turned out.

The bell dinged as Trevor entered the shop, still savoring

the irony. Yvonne was at the front counter and looked up from playing some sort of game on her phone when she heard the noise.

"Hey, Trevor." She smiled, and there was something knowing in that smile that he didn't like.

He silently vowed to make sure that she and Rachel never met.

"Owen's not in right now," she continued. "There was a problem with the fruit vendor. If there's anything on the news about a fistfight at the farmers market tonight, I'm officially pleading ignorance."

Trevor had been stomping the late January slush off his shoes on the doormat, but paused at her words. "The farmers market? You mean he gets his ingredients locally?"

"As much as he can. It's harder this time of year, of course, but—" She crossed her arms and over-exaggerated a frown. "If you're gonna do something, girlie, you might as fucking well do it right." She had deepened her voice as much as she could into what was a clear imitation of Owen's rumbling baritone. Trevor thought it a poor substitute.

"So now that the cat's away, what other secrets are you keeping from me? Is Owen always that friendly or am I just special?"

Instead of answering, Yvonne just looked at him. Again, Trevor was struck by her similarity to Rachel. Not physically, Yvonne being petite and dark where Rachel was taller, rounder, and blindingly pale against her red hair, although Trevor appreciated both of their physiques. When he went for women, either of them would be exactly his type, despite the fact they would both probably break him in half. Or maybe because of it. But their similarity was more in the way they seemed to look right through him, like they knew what he was about to say before he said it, and bought absolutely none of it.

No, they were definitely never allowed to meet.

"What can I get for you today?" Yvonne asked, pointedly changing the topic.

Trevor nodded. If that's how it was going to be, then fair enough. He respected her protecting her employer. He briefly wondered if that's all there was to their relationship, but quickly banished the depressing thought. Until proven otherwise, a man could hope.

Wait. What?

Trevor's forehead furrowed as he thought about it. He didn't actually want a relationship or anything like that with Owen O'Neill, did he? Sure, the man was attractive and Trevor had entertained more than one late-night thought about stripping him out of that apron and getting him all hot and bothered in a non-oven-related context, but that was it, right?

Yes, of course it was. Trevor didn't do relationships, and certainly not with any short-tempered, hot-headed pastry chefs, no matter how much his cookies made Trevor want to do unspeakable things, then curl up somewhere warm for a long nap.

So, it was just lust. That was fine, Trevor was definitely familiar with lust. In his opinion, lust wasn't even a conflict of professional interest. He'd slept with plenty of chefs, although it was difficult to be quite as excited by your bed partner once you'd been let down by their risotto. A hazard of his job, unfortunately. But he was just lusting after Owen, so it was nothing to worry about. One under-filled éclair and the feelings would vanish.

"Well?" asked Yvonne.

Trevor hummed, both in satisfaction at getting his personal confusion cleared up and in contemplation of the dessert case. He noticed that the cookies on display were all much smaller than the one Owen had given him the other day. Good. Every chef knew portion control was one of the key steps to profitability.

"I think perhaps something with less sugar this time. I do have to watch my girlish figure."

"How about some homemade breads?" Yvonne indicated the wall behind the counter, where a dozen different styles of loaves and buns were on display. "I could make you a selection of different rolls. The sourdough is especially popular. The starter was brought over by Owen's great-great-something grandmother when she immigrated back in the 1800s."

Trevor froze in the act of reaching for his wallet.

"How have the hipsters never found this place?" he blurted out.

Yvonne laughed. "Oh my God, can you imagine? Owen would have a coronary the first time someone asked if we had anything gluten free."

"Or with maple bacon."

"Or truffle oil."

"Or vegan."

Yvonne laughed again. She selected an assortment of half a dozen rolls and put them in the bag. "Did you want any butters or toppings?"

"Let me guess, he churns the butter from whole cream himself."

Yvonne didn't laugh.

"You're kidding me."

"I mean, I think he just uses a standing mixer but yeah,

has his own blend of different herbs and things he adds too." Yvonne shrugged. "Anyway, it's a dollar per two-ounce tub."

"I thought most places gave you one or two for free with purchase?"

"Most places probably do," Yvonne said slowly. "But most places can also afford an oven that isn't older than the staff."

Ah. Well, that explained a lot. Trevor had Yvonne add one tub of rosemary oregano spread and two tubs of salted honey butter to his order, then added a five to the tip jar. She nodded in thanks.

As he was walking out, he realized something.

"Wait," he said, holding the door for a pair of white-haired old ladies to enter. "Did you say 'an oven', singular?"

"See you next time, Trevor," Yvonne waved before turning to serve the women, greeting them by name.

Trevor nearly stumbled on the way back to his car as his mind raced over everything he'd learned. Well, he'd gotten the background information he'd wanted for his review. Shame he couldn't use any of it without his secret identity being revealed. He frowned. Yvonne would definitely figure it out if he used any of the specifics, and there was no way she wouldn't tell Owen. Maybe he could use the information and just never go back?

He sighed. No, there were enough angry chefs out there already. Even if Owen didn't hate him after the review, any one of them would be willing to offer good money if it got around that Owen knew Mr. Tasty's secret identity. From what Yvonne said, he'd pretty much have to take the money. After all, it wasn't like Owen owed him anything.

Trevor's stomach twisted unhappily at the thought. He opened the bag of rolls as soon as he sat down in his car and cranked the heater on. He was just despondent because he was hungry, that was all.

He reached for a tub of honey butter and the plastic knife Yvonne had tossed in. He'd try some of the rolls, jot down enough details to write his review, then never have to worry about Nana O'Neill's or anyone who worked there ever again.

CHAPTER 7

...the ambience of Nana O'Neill's lies somewhere between that of a sketchy bodega and the kitchen of that one grandparent your parents warned you to never ask about "The War".

But if anything, that only adds to the grubby charm of the place, making the confections to be found within true diamonds in the rough. The tartlets in particular shine like rubies and sapphires of cherry and blueberry decadence. Not to mention the Lebkuchen and slices of Schwarzwaldkuchen that would be enough to bring a smile to even that crotchety grandparent's face, as long as you never mentioned their country of origin.

And while we are on the subject of grubby charms...

* * *

"Oh my God. Owen, have you seen this?" Yvonne ran into the kitchen, still dressed in her coat and knit hat. Owen looked up from the piping bag. He'd zoned out while decorating little swirls and flourishes on the sugar cookies and must've lost track of time again.

"Seen what?"

"Oh my God." Yvonne grabbed his arm to pull him to his feet. Owen let her. "You have to see this! My sister texted me this morning saying she saw Nana O'Neill's in the newspaper..."

Owen jerked his head up. Fuck. Had some neighbor found

out about his past and filed a complaint? He cursed. He was well outside his probation period and the money he'd used to buy the bakery was his fair and square, but could he really prove that if he had to? Dammit, after all his hard work, was some stupid thing he'd done in his past really going to fuck him over now that he was just starting to earn an honest living?

Owen held his breath as Yvonne dragged him to the front of the bakery, expecting to be greeted by the blue flash of police car lights and two or three cops waiting out front, tapping their nightsticks against the glass.

There were definitely people waiting outside, but they sure didn't look like cops. And there were way more than two or three of them.

"The hell?"

"I don't know, I didn't have time to get the full story. Apparently there was a review? Owen, the line goes around the block! I had to fight my way through just to get to the door! Thank goodness you hadn't unlocked it."

Owen looked at the crowd of people, now starting to push and shove their way closer to the door. He looked over at his displays. He had enough baked already to make it through most of a normal day, but a crowd like this?

"I don't have enough."

Yvonne looked at him in astonishment, then glanced around, instantly sizing up the situation. "Okay, whatever's easiest and fastest to bake, go make that. Make as much of that as you can. I'll... I'll charge double for everything, maybe that will slow the herd."

Owen nodded and turned, before throwing one last quick glance out the front. "Five dollar surcharge for anyone with an undercut or Buddy Holly glasses. Taking pictures of the food costs ten dollars."

Yvonne laughed and Owen grinned as he ran back into the kitchen and grabbed his measuring cups. He didn't have time to wonder about this right now. It was time to bake his ass off.

* * *

Owen ran out of flour by noon. By three p.m., he'd sold the last of his flourless, egg-free, vanilla blondie bars. He brought a couple of bottles of beer over to where Yvonne was sitting at one of the small tables by the front window reading something on her phone. He'd had to shut the blinds when even the "Fuck off, we're CLOSED" sign on the front door hadn't stopped people from tapping on the glass or trying to wheedle their way in. The place was a mess and Owen wasn't even going to think about how late he'd be stuck cleaning up the kitchen, or all the emergency calls he still had to make to vendors before tomorrow. He just needed a minute to wind down first.

He kicked back in a chair and took a long drink. Damn, that hit the spot. Nothing like well-earned beer after a hard day of work. And this was probably the hardest day of work he'd ever had. He felt good. Exhausted, filthy, and sweaty, but good. Even closing early, they'd sold more today than they usually did all week. And with the frankly ridiculous prices Yvonne had been charging by the end?

He grinned around another sip. He could definitely afford more cake flour now.

"You've got to be kidding me!" Yvonne waved her phone at Owen. "I can't believe it! Owen, Mr. Tasty gave us a good review!"

"Mr. what?"

"Mr. Tasty. How have you never heard of him? Owen, he is *the* restaurant critic in Grand River. Everyone I know reads his column."

"That's a stupid name."

"No, you're missing the point. Mr. Tasty gave us a *good* review. The reason he's so popular is that he's an absolute asshole. He's vicious. He tears these restaurants apart and then people go to them just to say they've been. I've heard he literally gets death threats for the things he writes in his reviews, especially because they're all true."

"The fuck did he say about my bakery?" Owen growled, snatching Yvonne's phone from her hand. He squinted at the tiny font.

"That's just it, he loved Nana O'Neill's. I've only heard of him giving one other positive review before, and that was to Hubby Hogg's Bar-B-Que."

"Ain't that the barbeque sauce they sell at the grocery store?"

"Yes," said Yvonne. "Yes, it is. But it wasn't before Mr. Tasty reviewed it. Before that it was just a small joint down in southeast Grand River. Owen, this is huge."

Owen read more of the review. Positive? This dick called his bakery a "rundown, worn out mess, more homely than homey" and—

"The fuck does he mean by, 'If you're "lucky" enough to meet the owner and pastry chef, Owen O'Neill, you'll know. You would never think this pit bull-Humvee mix with the people skills of a poorly-trained grizzly would have the delicacy and precision to create such masterpieces.'?"

"Well, he's not wrong. Did you see where he called me 'a beacon of joy and ferocious beauty'? That's going on my Tinder profile."

"I'm going to kill him."

"Oh hush," she said, snatching her phone back. "From Mr. Tasty, that's basically a marriage proposal. Besides, you have other things to worry about. You want me to stay and help clean up?"

Owen downed the rest of the beer and leaned back, popping the joints in his spine as he stretched. "Just sweep up out here and head home. You can take everything in the tip jar too. You earned it."

Yvonne rolled her eyes. "I'm only not arguing because I have a thesis due and student loans. You know that right?"

"Yeah, yeah."

She stood up and gave Owen a friendly kiss on the cheek before grabbing both of their empty bottles and heading toward the broom closet. "If this keeps up, you'll be able to hire someone else to help out."

"Yeah, maybe."

CHAPTER 8

Outside on the sidewalk, Trevor slowed when he saw the closed shutters and huffed a laugh at the sign on the door. He raised his hand to knock anyway, then reconsidered. After the day he'd had, Owen was going to be in no mood to deal with Trevor, especially since it wasn't like Trevor could tell him he'd been the one responsible for all the business. Owen had earned it too. Every word Trevor had written was the absolute truth. That was one of the things he prided himself on as a critic.

He felt the corner of his mouth pull up in a smile and stopped. If anything, he should be annoyed with himself for sharing this place, rather than pleased with its success. Morals were so inconvenient. If only he was a little more selfish, he could have kept Owe—Nana O'Neill's all to himself.

Another week passed before Trevor went back to the bakery. It was one of the longest weeks of his life. Several foodie blogs had picked up on Mr. Tasty's "discovery" and reading their rave reviews had driven him to distraction. It wasn't just that they were obviously following in his footsteps, that was annoying enough, but the fact that other people were getting Owen's pastries when he wasn't pissed him off. Look at what everyone was saying about Owen's coffee cake, and he hadn't even tried it yet!

He managed to hold off going back until a few minutes before 5 p.m., not wanting to come any earlier and risk getting stuck in the crush of foodies and hipsters waiting ridiculous amounts of time in line just to be able to brag about the wait. If he was right, by now Owen would've figured out a new schedule too and shouldn't be closed early again.

His calculations were correct as always, and he was pleased to see that while there was a line, it was all firmly inside the bakery and not spilling out onto the street. Yvonne spotted him the moment he walked in.

"Trevor! Go ask Owen if he's done for today. I'm almost out of brownies and need to know if I should cross them off the menu."

"Good afternoon to you too," Trevor said as he walked around the end of the counter. Well, wasn't this a treat, being invited into the inner sanctum sanctorum. He didn't acknowledge any of those waiting in line but could feel their jealous glares at his back. Excellent. They should be jealous.

"So, this is where the magic happens," Trevor announced as he stepped into the kitchen. Wow, Yvonne hadn't been kidding when she talked about the age of the appliances. Everything looked like Owen must have gotten it third or fourth-hand, with the exception of a gleaming, top-of-the-line mixer that appeared to be brand new. For all the shabbiness of the kitchen, everything was impressively neat, each stand and pan clearly having its own place. Clean, too. Sure, it showed the wear of a full day's baking, but there was none of the ground-in food and grime that so many of Grand River's restaurants, even the most exclusive, had. A kitchen's cleanliness was a sign of a chef's dedication, and Owen was clearly exceptionally dedicated.

Trevor liked that in a man.

At the sound of Trevor's voice, Owen's head jerked up from where he'd been staring at a stack of ledgers and scattered papers with a yellow notepad under one elbow and a pencil tucked behind an ear.

"What are you doing back here?" he growled.

"Down, boy. I was invited in."

"Like a vampire," Owen grumbled, turning back to his papers.

Trevor laughed. "Exactly. Yvonne wants to know if you're baking anything else or if you're done for the night."

Owen rocked his chair back onto two legs as Trevor took the opportunity to step closer to see what he'd been working on.

"Kitchen's closed!" Owen boomed. He rocked his chair back onto all four legs, suddenly much closer to Trevor than he'd been before. Trevor tried to ignore the heat he could feel so close to his side as he examined the paperwork.

"Is this yesterday's balance sheet?" he asked, pointing at a page. Owen nodded. Trevor reached for another one of the ledgers and flipped through it. "Where's the rest of it?"

"What do you mean?"

Trevor looked up. "I mean, here in the debits column it just says, 'fruit guy $200'. Where's the itemization? Which fruits? How many of each? What were they for?" Trevor sat down on the edge of the table, ignoring the dusting of sugar as well as Owen's surprised expression. He flipped through another few pages.

"Owen, I don't see any sort of inventory and your profits column just has your daily take. Congratulations on that by the way, you should consider ways to reinvest in the business.

Wait, where are your recurring orders?"

"Recurring orders?"

Trevor looked up at the honest curiosity in Owen's voice.

"How do you keep track of what days your set orders are coming in from different vendors?"

Owen shrugged. "I don't? I just look around at what I have, and when I need new stuff, I order it."

"When you need new stuff..." repeated Trevor, flabbergasted. "You just keep all that in your head?"

Owen cracked his knuckles. "It's not that hard." His face darkened, "Or at least it wasn't until a week or so ago. Some hoity toity critic called my place sketchy and grubby like I should be ashamed of it. Asshole. If I ever find out who he is, I'm gonna show him what a pit bull-Humvee mix can do."

Owen glared off into the distance for a moment, then shrugged his shoulders, anger gone as quickly as it appeared. "I guess hipsters like that sort of thing though, since I've now got more of them than you can shake a stick at lining up to get in. It's like I'm a goddamn Apple store."

Trevor's heart sank. He'd meant sketchy and grubby in... Well, okay, not exactly in a *nice* way, but in a familiar way. Like a place that you knew so well you couldn't even see its faults. Still, it was probably for the best that Trevor's review had been nothing but unambiguously complimentary of Owen's pastries. At least that way there was no way Owen would ever think to link it to Trevor and his constant criticisms of his food. After all, he could never find out that Trevor was Mr. Tasty.

The pit bull-Humvee mix part was completely true, although perhaps said more about Trevor's personal tastes than could be considered entirely objective.

"I don't think you should be ashamed of your bakery,

Owen." Trevor added on quickly, "Even if some reviewer does."

That was close. He looked down at the papers in his lap. He'd learned enough about accounting during those mind-numbing business classes in college to know this was seriously complicated stuff and the fact that Owen was apparently keeping most of it in his head?

"I'm honestly impressed." Trevor hesitated. This wasn't any of his business, he was just here to grab a slice of coffee cake so his life could be complete. But his fingers twitched. He did love making things neat and tidy.

He spoke slowly, "If you want, I could have a look at this, maybe find a way to make it a little easier to keep track? I've done similar work before and might even find a way to save you a few bucks here and there."

After a moment of silence, Trevor looked up. Owen was sitting really, *really* close to him. When did that happen? He was also clearly thinking something through. Trevor waited, trying to still his hands.

"What's in it for you?" Owen finally asked.

Good question. Trevor didn't really want to examine why he was offering either, thank you. He glanced around.

"Pastries."

"What?"

Trevor smiled. "You can pay me in pastries. I'd hardly be the first person in the restaurant business to be paid under the table." Trevor was about to add more to that but caught himself in time. Fortunately, Owen didn't seem to notice.

Owen took a moment to consider. "Seems fair."

"Excellent." Trevor reached out and snatched the pencil from behind Owen's ear. As his fingertips skimmed across Owen's temple, he could almost have sworn he felt a slight shudder. It was probably just Owen flinching at someone in his personal space so suddenly. Trevor would react the same. He flipped to a new page in the ledger and started marking out some columns, studiously avoiding looking at Owen.

"I'll start with some of that coffee cake if you still have any," he said airily. "I hear it's passable. Not worth the wait in line, but passable."

Owen grumbled a few choice words under his breath. "Just come around the back next time."

When Trevor looked up, Owen appeared almost sheepish. It was an endearing look on him. He continued. "I keep it unlocked when I'm around anyway, and you're doing me a favor. So don't worry about the line, just come in the back. You can park there too, if you have a car. I won't have you towed. I know the meters..."

He trailed off. He didn't look at Trevor, in fact he was pretty obviously looking at anything *but* Trevor. Trevor couldn't help the small smile that stole across his face.

"Thanks," he said softly.

Owen grunted then cleared his throat. "I'll go see about that cake."

He walked out of the kitchen and Trevor's eyes followed for a moment, before he shook his head and turned back to the books.

CHAPTER 9

The next few weeks were some of the busiest of Owen's life. And some of the longest. Every morning he woke up earlier than the day before to bake increasingly huge amounts, but it seemed like they were selling out as soon as they came out of the oven. Between baking, decorating, and ordering supplies to bake and decorate more, he rarely got a chance to sit down until close, and then it was time to clean up before catching what few hours of sleep he could before starting all over again.

One morning, he came downstairs to the bakery hours before dawn, only to see a line had already started to form outside. He made up an extra pot of coffee and brought it out to the poor idiots waiting in the cold. It was the least he could do. They had to stay outside till Yvonne arrived, though. He wasn't going to let anyone in his shop while he was too busy to keep an eye on them. Except Trevor, of course.

He tried not to think about Trevor too much. That was easier said than done, but he at least tried not to think about *why* he tried not to think about Trevor too much. Or why he let him get away with so much either. If Owen was being honest, there was no way he could've kept up with everything without Trevor's help, but he barely even knew the man and he'd let him into his kitchen and his finances. Owen still wasn't sure which was more personal.

And in return, Trevor was a complete mystery to him. He

couldn't even figure out his schedule. Sometimes he came in first thing in the morning with a laptop and stole one of the prime tables in front, much to the annoyance of Owen's actual paying customers. Other times he came in a few minutes before closing just long enough to complain about Owen being a dinosaur who still did his books by hand before dropping off the ledgers and dashing off.

Then there were days like today, when he came in mid-afternoon and took over one of Owen's sorely needed kitchen counters for several hours. Sometimes while he worked on the books he chatted with Owen, nothing too personal or deep enough to distract either of them, and even hung around for a while after he was finished. Today he wasn't even working on anything, just reading a book with his long legs stretched out across half the kitchen like the giant inconvenience he was.

Owen should kick him out. He would. Later.

"You could do that out front," Trevor said without looking up.

Owen jerked, thinking he'd been caught staring. Trevor lowered the book and waved a hand at the rows of tiny chocolate leaves Owen was piping to decorate the mint chocolate mousse cups.

"You have that whole long counter up there, and Yvonne only uses part of it. You should use that space for your finishing work." Trevor grinned. "Give your customers dinner and a show."

Owen lifted an eyebrow, then raised an arm.

"I think I'm more likely to put them off their food." He went back to piping the leaves. He wasn't ashamed of either his tattoos or his scars, he accepted them for the reminders they were, but he still didn't want to see the revulsion in anyone's eyes. In Trevor's eyes.

Trevor scoffed. "Every chef I've ever met has tattoos. No one's going to be shocked. You know, you're really not so different from those hipster kids you pretend to hate. At least you don't have any truly awful ones that I can see. No skulls with crossed forks and spoons underneath or 'Live Fast, Eat Well' wrapped around a butcher's knife."

Owen snorted. "Watch your mouth. I've got an egg beater right over my heart."

Trevor's eyes widened, and Owen could see the apology forming on his lips, before he snapped his mouth shut and narrowed his eyes.

"No, you don't."

"Sure do." Owen forced down a grin. "I've got 'Live to Bake, Bake to Live' running down either side of my spine too."

Trevor still squinted at him, but didn't sound certain. "You're lying."

"You'll never know." Owen set down the piping bag and pushed his sleeve up further. "This one's pretty awful though."

It was one of the first one's he'd ever gotten, a strand of barbed wire circling his bicep that he'd paid a whole carton of cigarettes for. The sharp spikes had already blurred into gray blobs.

Trevor wrinkled his nose. "A timeless classic."

Owen laughed. "What about this one?" He pointed to a skull further down his arm. At least, it was supposed to be a skull. "I'll give you fifty bucks if you can tell me what this is."

"I like the snake above it," Trevor said instead, avoiding the question. "The colors are so vibrant."

"Thanks. I was on a six-month waiting list to get that one. Probably not my smartest choice though."

"Oh?"

"It's a coral snake, pretty deadly. Not the sort of thing people want to see when you're handing them food."

Trevor laughed, and Owen took a moment to enjoy the sound. He didn't make a habit of letting people see his tattoos, and he certainly didn't show them off, but the terrible ones were just as important to him as the ones that cost more than he could afford. They told the story of who he was, even if he'd never found someone who he wanted to read it.

"Besides, it's not just the poisonous tattoos." Owen rubbed at the ridge of twisted skin that ran down from his shoulder, ending just above the barbed wire. "It's the scars too."

Even as he said them, the words shattered his good mood with the memory of breaking glass and twisting steel.

Idiot. Why had he brought his scars up? It wasn't like Trevor could've missed them, he'd seen Owen in t-shirts enough times, and the one on his neck was impossible to cover unless he wanted to risk his life by wearing some of Trevor's ridiculous scarves while bending over a hot stove or whirling mixer. At least Trevor had never seen the full extent of them; that mess would put anyone off their food.

Another one of the things Owen tried not to think too much about was the fact he'd let Trevor see him in a t-shirt at all. He only wore them on days when Yvonne was working and he could mostly stay in the kitchen where wouldn't have to see people or let people see him, but somewhere along the way, Trevor stopped counting as *people.* That was troubling, but he already let the man lounge all over his kitchen. That was far more personal than seeing a bit of skin, even if that skin was literally covered with the proof of all his past mistakes.

Still, that didn't mean Owen had to draw attention to them.

He waited in the silence for Trevor to ask the inevitable.

"Is that chocolate mousse?"

Owen let out a bark of a laugh. "Yeah, mint chocolate actually."

Trevor, curious, tenacious, annoying-as-hell Trevor, had let the matter of his scars drop. Owen wasn't sure of the exact word for how that made him feel—something warm and fluttery—but he appreciated it, and let the warmth melt some of his concerns about the dessert at hand.

His nana's recipe was just for plain chocolate mousse, but Owen had thought it wouldn't be so bad to add a little creme de menthe for a bit of a grown-up kick. It tasted alright to him, but there still hadn't been a single thing Trevor tried that he didn't find *some* fault with. By now, he was pretty sure Trevor was just doing it to be a jackass—after all, he still ate the damn things. But this was his first attempt at his own recipe, and he wasn't sure he could bear to hear how bad it was.

"Well," said Trevor, "where's mine?"

Jerk.

"Fine." Owen selected one of the more lopsided cups, because if Trevor wasn't paying for it, he didn't get the belle of the ball. He carefully pried up two of the chocolate leaves that had already set and arranged them just so on top. The mousse itself was in a fragile chocolate cup that he'd made earlier, so he placed it on a plate to keep it from melting in his hands.

"Here you are, *sir*," said Owen, voice dripping with sarcasm even as his heartbeat picked up speed. "I hope it lives up to your standards."

He crossed his arms and waited. Trevor turned the plate and examined every angle of the mousse, then leaned in close and waved a hand like he was wafting the smell of it toward him. Owen rolled his eyes.

"Just eat the damn thing."

Elegant as ever, Trevor picked the cup up and took a bite. Like always, he closed his eyes as he chewed. The sweep of those dark lashes against his cheeks made Owen's heart beat even faster. Trevor was just so damn beautiful it hurt. He took another bite and Owen tensed. The suspense was killing him, so of course the asshole was drawing it out as much as possible.

He finally cracked. "Well?"

Trevor opened his eyes and slowly licked his lips. That was an image Owen would be saving for later.

"It's a little chocolatey."

Owen stared at him. "It's mint chocolate mousse. In a chocolate cup. With chocolate on top," he grit out.

Trevor shrugged. "I like the mint. But it was too chocolatey." He ate the last bite and licked the smears of chocolate off his fingers with a satisfied little noise. If Owen wasn't about ready to beat him to death, he'd be helplessly turned on.

Instead, he grabbed a roll of parchment paper and the pastry bag of warm chocolate.

"Where're you going?" Trevor asked.

"Out front. You wanna keep all your teeth, stay back here."

Trevor's laughter followed him out of the kitchen.

❋ ❋ ❋

"Here."

"Why do I always get the ugly, rejected ones?"

"To match your face. Now eat it."

"...Well, the flavor matches the exterior at least."

"Is that a smartass translation for 'it sucks'?"

"It is."

"Translate this: Go fuck yourself."

* * *

"What's this?"

"King cake. For Mardi Gras."

"Well, it's certainly colorful."

"Just eat the damn thing, Hill."

"...Too bland. Also, someone's going to choke on the plastic baby and die."

"If only."

* * *

"And?"

"The crust is acceptable, but you were too heavy handed with the nuts."

"Too many nuts. In a pecan pie."

"Exactly."

"Get out of my kitchen."

* * *

"Needs more vanilla."

"Yeah, yeah."

"No, I'm being honest this time, Owen. Taste it yourself."

"Huh."

"See?"

"So, does this mean you were lying all those other times?"

"Of course not. I've never said anything needed more vanilla before."

❊ ❊ ❊

"I don't know if these are any good. I don't think the new fryer cooks hot enough."

"It cooks at the temperature it says it's cooking at. You're just used to that deathtrap you used to have.

"It worked fine."

"It was a timebomb. As is this beignet. I can feel my arteries hardening already, although the diabetes may take me first. Tell them to bury me in the shade."

"So, more powdered sugar?"

❊ ❊ ❊

Trevor hummed happily to himself as he pulled into his spot next to Yvonne's beat up Honda Civic. He knew Owen didn't own a car. Based on the first pages of the ledgers in his passenger's seat, Trevor was pretty sure that was due to financial reasons, not city dweller reasons. Although if the numbers Owen had been pulling the last few months kept up, that wouldn't be a problem for much longer. He had an even better idea though: a delivery van. If Owen had one, he could do large orders, special deliveries, maybe even wedding cakes. Then a year or two down the line, catering, or a second location. He'd have to hire on more staff of course, but that shouldn't be a problem if—

Trevor's phone chimed, pulling him out of his daydreams. He shook his head. It was one thing to look over some figures for Owen; some people liked sudoku or the *Times* crossword, Trevor liked numbers. But planning out an entire business strategy for a friend?

Wait, he and Owen were friends? He rolled the word over carefully in his mind. He didn't really have friends. There was Rachel of course, but she was also his boss. He had colleagues and acquaintances, but Owen was certainly more than that.

"Friends" it was then. Unless there was a better word for "person whose livelihood you helped to flourish before you even knew them and didn't really like them anyway but now you do and continue to lust after them while berating their baking abilities because if you started telling them how amazing they actually are you might never stop."

Maybe in German. The Germans had a word for everything. His phone chimed again.

Follow up on my desk tomorrow or your ass is mine

Get more muffins

Trevor sighed. It'd been almost three months since his first review of Nana O'Neill's had been published, and Rachel had been on his ass for the last month at least to post a follow-up. It honestly shouldn't have been a problem. Most of the places Trevor reviewed had a week or two of better business just from being mentioned by him, then either went back to the numbers they had before, or shut down entirely. The very few who'd actually taken his criticisms and learned from them generally fared better after the initial rush died down, but he hadn't anticipated the success of Nana O'Neill's. Sure, that barbeque place he'd given his one other good review to had done well, but most of those franchise deals had already been in process, his review just gave them a little kick.

But Nana O'Neill's was just as busy now as it'd been the day his review came out. If anything, it was even busier. Owen complained about the line around the block getting longer every morning and being lucky they were selling as much as they did for all the free coffee he was handing out.

Which led to Trevor's current problem. Rachel wanted him to write a follow-up review of the hottest bakery in town. And Trevor wasn't sure he could.

It wasn't any concern about impartiality that bothered him. He could easily bang out a thousand words about how everything Owen touched turned to culinary gold and have it be nothing but pure, undeniable fact. The problem was that Trevor knew he wouldn't want to stop there. He'd want to talk about how hard Owen worked, how he used such outdated equipment but still managed to out-bake every other pastry chef in the city. How he'd laughed the first time Trevor had called him a pâtissier, because he had no idea how ridiculously, unimaginably brilliant he was, and how he pretended to hate anyone under thirty who came into his shop, but would let stressed college kids stay at the tables for hours and even sneak them extra cookies when he didn't think anyone was watching.

And Trevor couldn't say any of that, because if he did, he would lose it all.

Owen would never speak to him again if he found out Trevor was Mr. Tasty. He'd think Trevor had been lying this entire time just to get close to him for another review. He'd told Trevor things he certainly wouldn't have told a critic. He'd even let Trevor have his own parking space and let him wander into his kitchen whenever he wanted. Owen was his *friend*. He would hate Trevor if he knew who he really was.

Trevor gathered up the ledgers. He could do this. He could be a professional. It was all about compartmentalization. He would just go in, talk to Owen about some of the notations he'd made in the books, get Rachel her muffins and then go back to his office and write his completely unbiased, impartial review.

He took a deep breath and stepped out of his car.

"Owen?" he called out as he elbowed through the back door into the kitchen. "Are you intentionally paying too much for butter or do you owe a gambling debt to the dairy mafia?"

He looked around the kitchen. Empty. He dropped the ledgers on the nearest clean surface with a pout. He'd worked on that line all morning. He wandered toward the front of the bakery.

"Ow—" Trevor stopped in the doorway. He'd found Owen. And how.

Owen had apparently taken Trevor's advice about doing more of the kitchen work out front. He'd floured down the end of the counter and was kneading a large mass of bread dough. He rocked his entire body into the push-and-pull motion, large hands sinking into the dough before grasping and pulling it back, only to press forward again. He was in a long-sleeved shirt today, but it was threadbare and he had the sleeves rolled up to his elbows, hiding none of the flex of his powerful muscles as he worked. There was a smear of flour just above his jaw. A wave of emotion stronger than lust crashed over Trevor as he realized dizzily that he wanted nothing more in this world than to go over and gently brush the flour off.

"See something you like?"

Trevor turned his head just enough to see Yvonne out of the corner of his eye. She was smirking at him.

At that moment, Owen picked up the dough and dropped it

onto a tray, before nodding at the half dozen customers—male and female—who had crowded down the end of the counter to watch. He then raised his arms above his head in a full body stretch.

Trevor's mouth went dry. After a long moment, Owen dropped his arms with a grunt. He grabbed the tray and turned toward the kitchen. The moment he saw Trevor, his eyes lit up and he smiled.

"Hey, Trev."

Trevor turned around and walked out.

It wasn't until he'd been staring at a blank Word document for three hours that he realized he'd forgotten Rachel's muffins.

CHAPTER 10

...and those are just the pies. While Chef O'Neill continues to stick to the traditional classics, many of his pastries and desserts far outshine any other to be had in this city. To find the equal of a select few, such as his croissants and profiteroles, I suspect an international flight might be involved, although perhaps not even then.

But I may be unfairly biased in this regard. In all fairness, I must admit that I've easily visited Nana O'Neill's far more often than any other restaurant I've reviewed and find myself only more deeply entranced by the offerings there as time goes on. I must admit that this fondness may have spilled over into my appreciation of other aspects of Nana O'Neill's as well. As the increasing number of customers can attest, the unprepossessing decor and limited beverage selection tends to grow on one after a while. Even the surly owner himself is not without his charms...

❋ ❋ ❋

Owen threw an arm over his eyes and leaned back in his chair with a smile. He could hear Yvonne humming to herself as she emptied the cash register, some little pop tune he'd caught bits and pieces of, but didn't know the lyrics. What a goddamn *perfect* day. He'd known something was up when he made his first pre-open round of coffee and the line out front already stretched around the corner.

He'd called Yvonne to get in early and the next seven hours were nothing but a blur of measuring, whisking, and cooling. At some point Yvonne had swung into the kitchen and dropped off the lifestyle section of the *Chronicle.* Owen had glanced at it just long enough to see the name "Mr. Tasty" on the front page, with the words "Continued on page 4" at the bottom.

They'd sold out by noon.

He grinned and hummed along with Yvonne. Damn tune was catchy. He raised a bottle of beer to his lips and took a long pull. Only one thing could make this day better.

"Anybody home?"

"Out here!" Owen boomed. *Now* the day was perfect. He dropped his arm just in time to see Trevor walk into the front from the kitchen, a small smile on his face and the ledgers under one arm. It'd finally warmed up enough for him to lose those fancy coats, and the tight sweater he wore hinted at a trim, lithe figure underneath. Damn. If Trevor could look that good still covered neck to ankle, Owen wasn't sure he'd be able to handle it when the summer heat forced him to show a little skin.

Maybe he could convince Trevor to strip down under other, even hotter circumstances. He snickered.

"What are you laughing at?"

"A bad joke," Owen replied. "It's too awful even for you."

Trevor rolled his eyes and set the books on the counter. "Good day, I take it?" he asked Yvonne.

"Owen here, or should I say 'the Vulcan of the bread oven', got another write-up by Mr. Tasty. Another good one!"

"Congratulations. I assume this has something to do with why the blinds are closed?"

"Shh, if they hear you, they'll want cake. So, so much cake," sighed Owen happily. Then a thought occurred to him and he frowned. "No one saw you come in, did they? I had to chase two out already. They can't run so fast in their skinny jeans."

He eyed Trevor. Come to think of it, those jeans Trevor wore were pretty damn tight themselves. He leaned back further trying to get a better view. His chair wobbled on two legs and he flailed wildly before it finally settled itself firmly back down onto four. Trevor and Yvonne were both laughing at him, but he could forgive them. He took another drink; after all, it was a perfect day.

Trevor nodded toward the beer bottles littering Owen's table. "I take it the party started without me?"

"Better party now that you're here, Trev," Owen said. Well, "slurred" might have been a better word, but it had been a long time since he'd had one too many because he was in a *good* mood.

The cash register dinged as Yvonne closed it.

"And that's my cue to leave," she said. She walked over to Owen and handed him the zippered pouch containing the bills and change from the day's take. The zipper was straining to stay closed. "Here, don't spend it all in one place."

Owen fumbled a few bills out of the pouch without counting and pressed them into her palm.

Trevor's voice came from behind them. "You have absolutely no business sense, you know that right?"

"You want some?" Owen asked, holding out the pouch. "Tell me how to spend it. You were so clever about the new mixer and fryer and ramekins. So clever. Ain't he clever, Yvonne?"

"Yes, yes, Trevor's clever," she said. Owen snorted and Yvonne leaned down and kissed him on the cheek. "But don't listen to everything he says."

Owen drained the last of his beer as she walked away. He knew Trevor was lying about his crusts not being buttery enough if that's what she was worried about. He heard her say to Trevor, "He's all yours," as he reached for the rest of the six-pack on the table and popped the tops off the last two beers. He took his time with them so Yvonne could leave before he got them open. If she was gone, it was just him and Trevor.

Owen smiled to himself as he used brute strength to separate the metal caps from the cool, slick glass. Maybe, if he played his cards right, he and Trevor could find the perfect way to end the perfect day.

He turned to Trevor, outstretched beer in hand, but the invitation to join him died on his lips when he saw the look on Trevor's face. He looked like a kid who'd just found out Santa wasn't real and he owed the Tooth Fairy interest.

"You okay?" Owen asked.

Trevor straightened. "Fine," he said stiffly. "I just remembered an appointment. I only came by to drop these off anyway."

He dropped his eyes to the floor and waved a hand at the ledgers on the counter. He started to walk back toward the kitchen, then paused. Without turning around he said quietly, "Owen, I want you to know that you've earned every bit of your success."

And with that, he was gone.

Owen lowered both beers back onto the table. That was not how he was hoping this afternoon would go. Was it something he said? Or did? Fuck, had he been too obvious? He must've made Trevor uncomfortable.

He scrubbed his face with both hands. He might as well

go find the mop. His tired and aching muscles protested the movement. At least he'd be able to get a full night's sleep tonight. He couldn't remember the last time he'd gotten that. Of course, if Trevor had wanted to keep him from sleep...

But no, it was pretty clear that Trevor wasn't interested in that and Owen wasn't the kind to mope about things he couldn't have. Much.

Although he still wished Trevor hadn't run off so quickly. Owen hadn't even gotten a chance to tell him that his croissants were called the best in the US and maybe the world. Suck it, France.

CHAPTER 11

Trevor stopped with his hand just inches from the doorknob. It'd taken him almost a week to guilt himself into coming back. He'd thought he had a chance with Owen and he'd been wrong. Clearly. It happened every day and he was a grown man, he wasn't going to sulk about it. Just because he hadn't gotten that vibe from Owen and Yvonne at all, that was his fault for not paying enough attention. After all, people didn't just go around kissing their bosses. He should've picked up on the signs before he'd gotten his hopes up.

But Owen was his friend, dammit, and Trevor liked Yvonne. He was going to be happy for them, and supportive, and do everything he could to keep his emotions to himself and never let Owen know how Trevor felt about him. He wasn't going to lose his friend over something as trivial as his *feelings*.

It wasn't like anything could ever happen between them anyway. Not with the whole "Mr. Tasty" thing. He liked both his professional objectivity and his face exactly as they were, thank you.

He took a deep breath to steel himself and opened the door.

The sight that met him was a surprise. He'd gotten up early to come to the bakery before it opened. He knew Owen would already be there, elbows deep in the first round of the day's baking, but Trevor had figured it would be quieter then, and he could apologize to Owen for running out on him without anyone else around.

Without Yvonne around, whispered a petty part of him, but Trevor tried to ignore it. He figured he could spend an hour or two helping out to make amends, maybe even running coffee out to those in line, although his stomach roiled at the idea of having to interact with Owen's fans. But it was the least he could do after dropping off Owen's paperwork only half-finished and then bolting.

But the expected sight of freshly baked cookies and trays of scones and rolls ready to go in the oven was not what greeted him.

The kitchen was cold, no heat rising from the oven or stovetop to fill the air with the smell of baking pastries or bubbling fillings. It was quiet too, no whir of the mixers or even the quiet hum of Owen singing to himself. On the counter there was a covered bowl that Trevor knew meant rising bread dough, but that was it. No other doughs, no finished desserts, no Owen.

"Owen?" He asked cautiously as he stepped in. Had something happened to him? Had there been a break in, or had he gotten hurt with no one around to help or—

"Owen!" Trevor yelled louder.

"Mmph?"

The noise came from the walk-in pantry and Trevor sprinted to it, fearing the worst. For a terrible moment, all his worst fears were confirmed when he caught sight of Owen slumped in the far corner. His heart stopped in his chest as all the things he'd never had a chance to say caught in his throat.

He already had his phone out to dial 911 when his brain caught up with the rest of him. As he took full stock of the situation, his heart juddered to a start again and he let out a shaky breath.

On closer inspection he could see that Owen wasn't injured at all, just asleep. He was sitting on a pile of flour sacks in the corner, passed out with his head tipped back against the wall, hands slowly clenching and unclenching in his sleep like a cat. His apron hung loosely around his neck, untied, looking like a comically small blanket draped over his massive frame.

A giant and his blankie.

Trevor's shouts must not have really roused him, because his lips were open and he was snoring softly, a small puddle of drool forming in the corner of his mouth.

A smile tugged at the corner of Trevor's mouth as he knelt down next to him, and let himself take a long look. *Just for a minute.*

Owen was beautiful like this, the peace and quiet so unlike the intense energy and overwhelming presence Trevor was accustomed to. He smiled as he watched Owen's hands move. Even in sleep, Owen couldn't be perfectly still, the same way even when he wasn't working, he always had to be fiddling with one of his appliances or running a rag down the counter.

His eyelashes swept down over his cheeks and Trevor hadn't noticed until now how absurdly long they were. He reached out, then stopped himself, his hand an inch above Owen's face. Dammit, this was exactly what he'd told himself he *wouldn't* do.

He redirected his hand to Owen's shoulder and gave him a light shake. When this only made him snore louder, Trevor shook him again, harder.

"Wakey wakey."

"Huzzuh?" Owen mumbled. He blinked, eyes soft and unfocused before zeroing in on Trevor. "Trev?"

Oh fuck, Trevor was doomed. At seeing Owen like this, peaceful, quiet, and vulnerable, all the walls he'd built came crumbling down. His sarcasm, his sneers, his snobbery, what was the point of any of that if it kept Owen at a distance, when all Trevor wanted was to get as close to him as possible? He wanted to be allowed behind Owen's snarling facade the way he was allowed into his kitchen. To be the one who got to see the traits of warmth and kindness Owen kept so deeply buried, sometimes Trevor wasn't certain he even knew he possessed them.

He'd been attracted to Owen the moment he first laid eyes on him, but he knew his feelings had progressed far beyond that. The man was beautiful the way a mountain or a raging river was beautiful, powerful and unstoppable. He was an artist as well, with a skill for baking that frustrated Trevor, because no matter how many reviews he wrote, he wasn't sure he could ever capture Owen's genius on the page. Not that Owen believed Mr. Tasty's praise at all.

And that was the problem right there. It was hard enough to continue to keep his secret, something inside him begging him to come clean. But Trevor had never been the sort of person to do things by halves. If he told Owen the truth about how he felt, the truth about the rest of it would come tumbling out as well. Trevor would be risking his secrets, his job, everything he'd spent a lifetime building. No matter what he might feel, for his own sake, he had to keep Owen at arm's length.

And when had they gotten so close anyway? He stood up quickly and took a few steps back.

"I came in this morning to apologize, and found you *sacked* out back here." Trevor brushed some non-existent dust off his pants while Owen got his bearings. Then because he'd never been one to take his own advice, he stuck a hand out to help Owen up. If he was damned anyway, he might as well enjoy the suffering.

Owen grasped Trevor's outstretched arm by the wrist and together they pulled him to his feet. Trevor thrilled at the feel of Owen's warm skin under his palm, the strength in his shifting muscles under the tattoos. He hoped Owen didn't notice the shiver that ran through him when Owen wrapped his fingers around Trevor's wrist, or how close they were now standing. Owen still seemed a little out of it though, so he probably didn't. Trevor understood, he wasn't at his best first thing in the morning, either.

"Apologize? For wha—oh fuck!" Owen pushed past Trevor into the kitchen. He looked around at the bare counters and then at the clock on the wall that read 6:22 a.m.

"Oh fuck, fuck, *fuck!*"

Trevor stepped quickly to the side to avoid being bowled over as Owen ran back into the pantry and threw a fifty-pound sack of sugar and another of flour over either shoulder like they were nothing.

"Oh fuck. Okay, cookies? Cookies are fast. Fuck it, today's cookie day. Where's the coffee? Oh fuck!"

The sack of flour went crashing to the floor, splitting along a seam and releasing a white cloud into the air. Coughing, Trevor could just about make out Owen throwing the bag of sugar down on the counter, then clutching his shoulder through a barrage of expletives. He didn't just sound panicked now, he sounded like he was in pain.

"Owen? Owen!" Trevor shouted. He stepped forward at the same time Owen turned, and caught Owen's upraised elbow right to the face.

His vision went white—some combination of flour cloud and the explosive pain. He took a step back, realizing his mistake as his foot slipped in the thick layer of flour. Adding insult to injury, he banged his head on the counter on the way down.

"Ow?" he said from the floor, dazed.

Owen was immediately by his side.

"Oh fuck, Trev, are you alright? Oh Jesus, you're bleeding. Fuck. Hold still."

Trevor watched as Owen whipped the apron off over his head with a hiss of pain before holding it under the sink and soaking it in cold water. Trevor touched his fingertips to his nose. It didn't feel broken, but when he ran his fingers across his upper lip, they came away red. He gingerly touched the back of his head. No blood there, thank God, but he could already feel the beginnings of a pretty bad goose egg.

Owen was by his side again, one hand darting out toward Trevor's face with the wet apron. Trevor flinched and instinctively slapped his hand away.

"Oh fuck, Trev. I'm so sorry. Fuck." Owen dropped the apron and scooted back. Trevor pinched his nose to halt the flow of blood, then picked the apron off the floor and held it to his face, ignoring the flour already caked to the fabric.

"Owen?" said Trevor, when the blood had finally slowed to a trickle.

"Yeah, Trev? Fuck, I'm sorry. What can I do?"

"Say 'fuck' one more time."

Trevor looked over at Owen just in time to see his face go from anguish, to shock, to absolute disbelief.

"*Fuck* you."

"Thank you." Trevor couldn't help it—he started laughing. The laughter made his nose start to bleed again, and perversely, that just made him laugh even harder. He laughed until his ribs hurt, and when he finally started to subside, he looked at the absolute carnage all around them and that just set him off again.

"I'm a snow angel," he finally gasped.

"How hard did you hit your head?"

Trevor snorted. "Ow, fucking, ow." His nose finally seemed to have stopped bleeding, but his navy pullover and Owen's apron were both covered in a disgusting mix of blood and flour.

"I hope you have another apron. This one isn't sanitary. Plus it might worry the customers."

"Oh fuck, the customers," Owen said. Trevor couldn't help his small giggle. It'd been an emotional few days.

Owen glared at him, then looked shamefaced for doing so. He handed Trevor a wad of damp paper towels with a sigh. "I'm supposed to open in half an hour and all I have is one batch of ciabatta dough made up, a huge fucking mess, and you bleeding out in the middle of my kitchen."

Trevor dabbed at his face and neck with the towels, careful of his sore nose. "So don't open."

"I can't just not open. I've been open every day for the last two years."

"Sure you can. You're the hippest eatery in all of Grand River right now. You being closed is only going to make the foodies love you more. Makes you exclusive."

Owen still looked uncertain, so Trevor pressed on. "You did something to yourself, didn't you? That's why you dropped the flour. You pull a muscle?"

Owen shook his head. "Old injury. Same one as this." He

tapped the scar that ran up from the collar of his henley, leaving behind a floury mark on his neck that made it difficult for Trevor to focus on his words. "Bad car wreck."

Owen plucked his shirt, releasing a plume of flour. "The doctors did a good job stitching me back together, but you wouldn't want to see the mess under this."

Trevor strongly disagreed, but it wasn't time to get sidetracked. "You haven't had a problem carrying things before."

"Yeah well, *before* I needed more than one hand to count the number of hours of sleep I'd gotten in a week."

"Is that why you were passed out in the panty?"

Owen sat down hard on the floor, his injured arm cradled in his lap. He leaned back against the counter across from Trevor. When he stretched his legs out, their feet tangled together.

Trevor gave him a light kick when no answer seemed to be forthcoming.

"Just tired is all. Shoulder will be fine once I get a chance to rest it." Owen closed his eyes as he spoke. "Don't get me wrong, I'm happy to finally be making some money with this place, but with all the baking and then the cleaning, organizing, ordering... I was up late working on the books too. You're right, I need to get that computer program, your handwriting is shit."

"No, it's not," Trevor said reflexively, then frowned. "Wait, I knew you did the orders and inventory, but I assumed Yvonne did the cleaning at least, or you called someone else in?"

"No, you know Yvonne's in grad school, some kinda science thing I don't understand. She doesn't have time for that. Yesterday was her day off anyway, since until recently, Mondays were always quiet. I guess I just got used to it."

"And you do this seven days a week?"

"Mm-hm…"

Owen drifted off even as he spoke. Trevor stared at him incredulously. It wasn't possible. The kind of hours Owen must be pulling every single day? For years?

Trevor stood up cautiously, careful not to kick Owen or give himself another head injury in the process, but aside from a slight throb his head felt fine. He went over to the sink and washed the remaining blood off his face and hands. He tried dusting the flour off his clothes, but the addition of damp hands only made the mess worse. He was sending Owen his dry-cleaning bill. He could afford it now.

Grimacing at himself, he took a moment to put the dough in the refrigerator. He had no idea if that would ruin it, but he had other things to worry about. Ignoring the dusty footprints he left behind, he walked through the bakery and unlocked the front door.

The crowd outside rustled as the door opened and Trevor even heard a cheer or two from the back. He looked at the person at the front of the line. The kid was narrating something to his phone, a pair of AirPods sticking out from underneath a wool beanie, and clearly nothing better to do than wait three hours to buy baked goods.

"We're closed. Come back tomorrow." Trevor shut the door on the kid's protests and re-locked it. Almost immediately, knocking started on the door, but he ignored it.

Once back in the kitchen, he stepped over Owen to get to the wall phone and looked at the list of numbers pinned beside it. Sure enough, right there between "Dairy Asshole" and "Sugar Guy" was Yvonne's name and number. Her name was written in a much clearer, more feminine hand than all the others, for which he was grateful, because if Owen thought he could give Trevor shit about his handwriting?

Trevor smiled as the phone on the other end rang.

"Hey, Owen! Need me to pick up something on my way in?"

Trevor swallowed. Of course Yvonne assumed it was Owen, it was his bakery after all. No reason to feel disappointed at the cheer in her voice.

"No, it's Trevor. Trevor Hill?"

There was a long silence. He tried not to feel nervous.

"I know who you are, Trevor. Why are you calling from the bakery? Is Owen okay?"

"He's fine," said Trevor. "Just overworked. We decided not to open Nana O'Neill's today so he could get some rest. I wanted to let you know before you drove in."

The silence was back. "Really? You decided that together?"

"Well," Trevor looked down at the sleeping Owen at his feet. The little hand movements were back. Cute. "*I* decided and I'm sure Owen will agree with my decision when he wakes up."

Yvonne laughed. "Sure he will. Thanks for the heads up, Trevor. Don't be a stranger."

"Wait!" said Trevor before she could hang up. He glanced down, but Owen hadn't even flinched. "Did you want to come get... I mean, he's your... I don't even know where he lives!"

Yvonne laughed at him again. "Nope. He's your problem now, have fun with that."

Trevor could almost swear there was a leer in her voice, but before he could say anything else, she hung up on him. He put the phone back in its cradle, then took out his phone and added her number to his contacts. Just in case.

He looked down at Owen. Okay, get him home and make sure he got to bed, just like any friend would do. How hard could it be?

Trevor knelt down and shook Owen's good shoulder. "C'mon, up and at 'em." He purposefully looked away this time as Owen woke up. He knew his limits.

"Mmmgh. Fuck, gotta bake..." Still half asleep, Owen struggled to get up. Trevor pressed on his uninjured shoulder to hold him down and was frankly shocked when instead of just swatting Trevor aside like he was definitely strong enough to do, Owen relaxed into his grip instead.

"Hey, hey, we've been through this," Trevor said. He rubbed small, soothing circles with his thumb at the point where the collar of Owen's henley met his skin, purposefully keeping his mind away from what he was doing even as his fingers itched to do the same on the other side of Owen's neck to see if the scar there felt any less warm than the rest of him.

"No baking today. You're taking a vacation. And before you say anything else, I've already called Yvonne and informed the crowd out front, so you don't really have a choice." He cocked his head, thinking. "Unless you want to try to run this thing with no goods, no cashier, and no customers?"

"Well, when you put it like that," Owen grumbled.

Trevor pulled his hand back reluctantly and stood up. "I knew you'd see it my way."

He started straightening the ledgers on the counter so he'd have a reason not to look at Owen as he said the next part. "Just because I'm such a good friend, I'll give you a ride home as well. Can't have you passing out on the subway, can we?"

"Okay."

Trevor's heart leapt when Owen didn't say anything to correct his "friend" assumption. He viciously fought to keep down his grin.

"But it's not much of a drive. I live upstairs."

"Upstairs?"

"Yeah, the place came with a one-bedroom apartment upstairs." Owen groaned as he got to his feet, then scratched his chin sleepily. "At least, it's a one-bedroom now. It was a studio, but I threw up a couple walls. You can come see if you want."

Owen grabbed a key ring off the hook by the back door that Trevor had been wondering about. He followed Owen and when they were both outside, Owen locked the kitchen door behind him before going a few steps over to a metal door with peeling blue paint and unlocking two sets of locks. When the door opened, Trevor peered around him to see a long flight of stairs leading up into the darkness. Owen flipped a light switch just inside the door and started up.

"It's not much…"

Trevor didn't care how much it was, he was overwhelmed with curiosity. Based on the overall age and appearance of Nana O'Neill's decor, he'd assumed that Owen lived in an old house somewhere on the edge of Grand River. Somewhere clean but full of the same furniture that'd been there forever, maybe even the same house he'd grown up in.

Since there wasn't any mention of rent or mortgage in the ledgers, he knew Owen owned the bakery outright, but that he lived here as well? Trevor was so distracted he almost didn't notice that following Owen up the stairs put him right at eye level with his ass. Almost.

He took a quick moment to capture the image in his mind for later, then they reached the top of the stairs.

Owen's apartment was an absolute wreck. The space itself could generously be called open-plan and was relatively large, the same size as the entire storefront and kitchen below, but those were the only positive things that could be said about it.

To the right of the stairs was the saddest kitchen Trevor had ever seen. It made the worn-out kitchen in the bakery below look like something off of HGTV. The cabinets were three different designs, hopefully scavenged from a resale store and not a dumpster, although Trevor wasn't going to bet on it.

In the middle of the apartment was a fold-out card table flanked by two mismatched chairs that Trevor suspected constituted the formal dining area. To the left was what might be called a living room, but in reality was just a rug thrown down on bare floorboards with a sagging sofa facing a small TV.

The whole room was a mess. In front of the sofa where a coffee table should be, a couple of cartons sat covered in beer bottles and takeout containers. The sofa itself looked like Owen had just dumped his clean laundry on it when it was done.

Trevor wrinkled his nose. At least he *hoped* it was clean laundry.

Straight ahead was a long hallway flanked by walls with the apartment's only fresh paint and Trevor could see two open doors down the end.

"You *live* here?" Trevor couldn't keep the horror from his voice.

"Yeah well, we can't all have whatever fancy-ass townhouse or penthouse or whatever-house you live in," Owen said, without any real heat. "I've seen your nice car, don't deny it."

"I won't." Trevor had a condo, actually, but it was a very nice condo. He pointed at the hallway. "Wait, are those the walls you built? They look professional."

Owen shrugged. "Did some time on construction gigs here and there. It's not that hard once you know what you're do

—" He interrupted himself with a jaw-cracking yawn that set Trevor yawning himself.

"Sorry, I don't think I'm much up for entertaining." With that, Owen whipped off his shirt and started walking down the hall.

Trevor froze in place. Owen shirtless was everything he'd hoped it would be and more. He'd only gotten a quick impression of his chest and that impression was "Yes, please," but he stared at Owen's broad back as he walked away. The man was enough to make Michelangelo weep. The strongly defined muscles flexed as he walked, making the tattoos that spread across his entire back shift like living paintings.

He'd thought Owen had been joking about the extent of his tattoos, but apparently not. The man was covered in them. Trevor spotted a few gray skulls and basic outlines of daggers mixed in amongst brightly colored flowers and more snakes that looked real enough to slither.

However, some of the designs were less easy to make out. Curled over and around his shoulder, bands of scar tissue raced down his back like lightning bolts, twisting and deforming both the exquisite and the crudely drawn tattoos equally. In some places, running alongside the longer scars were smaller dotted ones he recognized as being from sutures. Other places were pitted with deep marks, like someone had tried to gouge the ink from his skin.

Trevor shuddered. Not at the appearance of the scars, but at how much pain Owen must have been in after the car crash from such terrible injuries. With shocking clarity, he realized how lucky Owen was to be alive at all.

Trevor was stuck on that thought so long he missed most of what Owen said next.

"...if you want before you go. It locks automatically. Thanks."

Owen disappeared through one of the open hallway doors into what Trevor assumed was the bedroom. He took an involuntary step forward and then scowled at himself. His head hurt and he's stayed longer than he meant to already. He should go.

As he turned, his eyes caught on the keys that Owen had tossed on the card table. His mind flashed to the mess left downstairs. He really shouldn't leave that for Owen to have to deal with when he woke up, and he knew where Owen kept the ledgers, the least he could do was bring those up so Owen didn't have to go back down to the bakery again later.

Or Trevor could take a look at them himself? It shouldn't take him too long to get caught up, and he'd been thinking of ways he might be able to find the budget for a second oven...

Trevor swiped the keys and headed down the stairs.

CHAPTER 12

Owen woke slowly and blinked at the late afternoon sun shining in through his window.

That can't be right—I'm never home in the... Oh, yeah.

He groaned as he rolled over onto his back, sheets tangling around his legs. God, he'd needed that nap. He was still groggy, still too behind on sleep to be fully caught up, but he felt a hundred times better than he had that morning.

His sleep cycle was going to be fucked though.

He winced. His sleep cycle wasn't the only thing that was fucked. Yeah, being closed a day probably wouldn't ruin his business, but he'd have an extra day's worth of ingredients that he'd have to subtract from his next orders, and wasn't that new dairy guy supposed to come by to talk prices?

Fuck. Maybe if Owen was really *really* lucky, when Trevor called Yvonne he'd seen the note and called the dairy guy to reschedule too.

Mmm, Trevor.

Owen slid a sleep-warm hand down his stomach and under the waistband of his boxers. He'd been conscious enough to kick off his jeans before collapsing into bed. Convenient. It would've been more convenient if he'd been conscious enough to invite Trevor to join him for his nap instead of just to see the apartment. Owen wrapped his fingers around his cock and pulled gently.

Yeah, now that would be something to wake up to, Trevor is his bed, all fuzzy with sleep, his perfect hair out of order and his sharp words dulled for once behind soft, parted lips.

Owen sped his hand up.

That was fine, there were plenty of things he and Trevor could do in a bed that didn't involve talking. He moaned at the thought. Trevor would probably do that cute little nose scrunch thing when he woke up that he did when the sun got in his face too. Damn, that was adorable.

Owen stilled his hand. What the fuck? It was one thing to get off thinking about how hot Trevor was, but to thinking he was *adorable*?

His cock twitched.

No, dammit. He pulled his hand out of his boxers. Those weren't the kind of thoughts you had about someone you just wanted to sleep with, those were... Those were something else.

He rolled up to sit on the edge of his bed, trying to ignore his hard on. It'd just been way too long, that was all. He had enough shit to deal with without trying to make his feelings for Trevor out to be more than they were. He just needed to get laid. Maybe in a week or two, when he was more settled into the new routine, he'd close early again. Take an evening off to find some company.

He nodded, plan settled. But first he had to take a shower, then see what he could salvage of the rest of the day. He waddled across the narrow hallway into the bathroom.

Better make it a cold shower.

A quarter of an hour later, refreshed and revived, Owen circled his shoulder in the bathroom mirror. Not back to normal yet, but it felt infinitely better than it had before. Satisfied, he popped a couple of ibuprofen, wrapped a towel around his waist, and wandered out into the main area of his apartment in search of food. There should still be some of that lo mein left in the fridge unless he'd—

Trevor was sitting at his dining table.

"Fuck!" Owen didn't jump back in surprise, but it was a close thing. "Jesus Trev, you nearly gave me a heart attack."

"Sorry." Trevor coughed. Christ, he looked almost as startled as Owen. "I was going to take a second to fix up the books but ended up taking a deep dive and lost track of time. I didn't mean to stay this long. I'll go."

"Don't worry about it," Owen said. His heart was still going about a hundred miles an hour, but he tried to play it off. "You'd just have to explain it to me later, anyway." He walked over to the fridge to see about leftovers, but was stopped by the sight of something on his counter. "What's this?"

"Ah."

No further explanation seemed to be coming.

"Ah?"

Trevor looked away. "I thought I could make up that bread dough you had downstairs—waste not, want not—I found a recipe online but I couldn't remember exactly what kind you said it was. It's harder to make than you'd think."

Owen laughed and Trevor glanced over at him, a quicksilver smile on his face, then looked away again.

"So anyway, I hope it was a flatbread, because it came out like a flatbread. It's edible but—look, can you go put some clothes on or something?"

And like that, the happiness that had been bubbling up in Owen burst.

Oh right. Yeah, he could do that. He'd find something with long sleeves too. No reason to put Trevor off more than he already had. Owen knew how awful his scars were; he wasn't going to subject Trevor to them any longer, especially after the guy had taken his whole day to deal with Owen's fuck ups, from his falling asleep on the job, to being unable to open the bakery, even to his damn paperwork. He'd even tried to salvage Owen's dough, although how he got a flatbread out of ciabatta Owen wasn't going to ask.

Feeling his cheeks grow warm with shame, he turned his back before Trevor could see—not that his back was any less fucked up than his front, and made his way over to the sofa to grab whatever pair of jeans and long sleeve shirt he could find in the pile.

"What happened to my pile?"

When he looked over his shoulder, Trevor was studying a stain on the table intently.

"Trevor, what happened to my pile of clothes?"

"My pants had flour all over them and my shirt was covered in blood. Obviously, I wasn't going to wear that all day, so I figured it would be alright if I borrowed something. I'll wash them before I return them, don't worry! But it was all such a mess that I may have... folded the rest?"

Owen looked at where his clothes were sitting on his coffee-table crates, neatly folded into precise stacks of shirts, pants, and boxers, with his socks folded together into matching pairs. The empty boxes and bottles that had been on and around the crates were long gone too.

Okay, a little creepy, but honestly? A man could get used to this.

His brain finally caught up with Trevor's explanation and he jerked his head up. Sure enough, the shirt Trevor was wearing was one of Owen's henleys. It was buttoned all the way up, but hung so loose on his slender frame, so different from Owen's own, that the collar gaped low and wide on his neck, revealing delicate collarbones and freckled skin halfway to the shoulder. Trevor was swimming in it, especially compared to the perfectly tailored tops he usually wore. He'd grabbed a pair of sweatpants too. Owen could tell which ones they were immediately; he'd had them for years and knew from experience they were buttery soft and worn-in just right. Even from across the room, he saw that they came up too high on Trevor's legs. He must've rolled them at the waist to counter the worn-out elastic. They'd still be far too big on him, just barely hanging off his slim hips. All Owen had to do was give them one firm tug.

Owen growled and grabbed the first pants and shirt he saw to keep himself from grabbing something else. He stomped into the bedroom to change and slammed the door hard.

Christ. There was only so much he could be expected to endure. He slipped the towel off. He'd forgotten to grab underwear, but there was no way in hell he could go back out there now. The pants he'd grabbed were a pair of baggy sweats that should hide most sins, but unfortunately the shirt was only a tank top. He worried the hem of it between his fingers for a moment, considering.

Fuck it. Trevor had already seen his scars and their constant reminder would do a better job of keeping Owen in check than his own admittedly weak self-control.

He caught a glance of himself in the mirror he had propped up against his bedroom wall and pointed at his reflection.

"Don't fuck this up."

With a deep breath, he walked out of the bedroom. He could do this.

"So what other life changes did you make while I was asleep?" he asked as he walked as calmly as he could into the kitchen. He couldn't help but notice the quick once-over Trevor gave him, followed by a look of relief that felt like a stab to the heart. Good. Thinking about that would keep Owen from doing anything stupid.

He grabbed a bread knife from the block and tried to cut into the flatbread. That didn't work. He grabbed the knife sharpener and tried again. Finally, he put the knife down and with effort, tore a piece off like that had been the idea all along.

He took a bite. Well, it was definitely bread. Technically. Burned on the bottom, rubbery on the top, and still raw in the middle, but bread. How was that even possible? He turned to find the trash can to spit it out, but caught Trevor's eye. Oh Christ, he looked so damn hopeful. Owen chewed for another minute and then swallowed.

"S'not bad," he said. Trevor's eyes lit up, and against his better judgment, Owen took another bite. At least if it killed him, Trevor knew where all the important paperwork was. Speaking of...

"So, life changes?"

"Oh!" said Trevor, attention immediately back on the books in front of him. "I found a couple of places where you can save money. Not much, but a few dollars every week are going to add up over time, especially considering your current increase in sales. We should talk about savings plans too. I also went ahead and ordered that software. I had it sent to the bakery since you'll be down there when they deliver it anyway."

"Thanks. Let me know what I owe you."

Trevor waved a hand. "Make more of those rhubarb souffles, they're alright. Here, let me show you what I did."

Owen grabbed the chair from the other side of the table and plopped it down next to him. Trevor spent the next two hours talking Owen through the changes he'd made to Owen's ordering system—"Yes, before you ask, I rescheduled with the new dairy guy."—and explaining the new twice-a-week system he'd set up for all the deliveries instead of having a couple of different ones delivered each day.

Unlike every other time someone tried to teach Owen something to do with numbers, Trevor didn't make him feel stupid at all. He had a way of explaining things that made sense, and even when Owen didn't get an idea right away, he found another way to lay it out and didn't get frustrated or annoyed if it took a couple of tries.

By the time they'd finished, the sky outside the apartment windows was darkening.

Trevor glanced at the time on his phone. "I guess I should be going."

"Wanna stay for dinner?" Owen asked, emboldened by his pride in everything he'd learned. At the uncertainty on Trevor's face, he backtracked. "You don't have to, if you have somewhere to be. I just figured you'd earned a free meal."

"No," said Trevor slowly. "No, I'd like that."

"Good." Owen huffed. "I'm still putting you to work though. You can boil water, right?"

Owen tried to hide his doubts at Trevor's exasperated eyeroll. After the bread, that had been a serious question.

He grabbed his keys from where Trevor had left them hanging from a nail that stuck out of the stair rail. That was actually a pretty great place for them. "Pots are over the stove. If I'm not back in ten, put the rest of the box of pasta in. Top shelf in the cabinet by the wall."

Downstairs, Owen unlocked the bakery and went into the kitchen. He took a second to marvel at it. There was still flour in the tile grout and along the baseboards, but the majority had been swept up, the bag itself folded over itself to contain the remaining flour and set neatly on the counter. It wasn't as good a job as Owen could do, and would only maybe pass a health inspection, but it would save him a lot of time in the morning.

A smile tugging at his lips, he walked over to the pantry. Most of what he needed was there. Some of the ingredients he had on hand for the pre-wrapped sandwiches that were popular in the afternoon, the rest were for the shepherd's pie he'd been thinking of trying. Most importantly, he made sure to grab the garlic, before getting some butter and minced lamb out of the refrigerator. He did a quick walkthrough to make sure everything was closed up for the night, then headed back upstairs.

When he got there, Trevor was just dumping the rigatoni into the boiling water. Owen should have told him to add a pinch of salt first, but too late now. He unloaded his armfuls of food onto the counter, then started the hunt for a saucepan.

"Can I help?"

"Sure, just a sec," said Owen, pulling out the pan and putting it over a burner on low. He poured just a splash of olive oil into it, before pulling out a wooden spoon and handing it to Trevor. "Once that heats up, add about half the lamb, then keep mixing it around so it cooks evenly."

Trevor nodded, and went to stand by the stove, eyes intent on the pan. Owen washed the vegetables and diced the pepper and onions. They were ready to go into the pan just after Trevor tentatively added the lamb.

"Good. Now keep stirring until the meat looks like

something you'd want to eat." Trevor nodded, and Owen cut up a couple heirloom tomatoes, before painstakingly slicing the bread Trevor had made in half lengthwise and placing both pieces on a large baking sheet. He coated the uncooked sides in a mix of butter and crushed garlic and carefully nudged Trevor out of the way so he could pop the whole thing under the oven broiler.

"Owen?"

Owen stood up and inspected the pan. The lamb looked just about perfect, so he turned the heat down to just the lowest simmer, before carefully adding the tomatoes and a handful of herbs.

"Be better if I had some mushrooms, but I don't bake with them much," he told Trevor. "Considering the lamb, I'd prefer pappardelle noodles too, but rigatoni will do."

Trevor looked a little dazed, so Owen took the wooden spoon from him and kept stirring. "Grab the colander out and put it in the sink. Get some plates down, too."

Trevor did, and just in time. Owen poured the rigatoni into the colander, then gave it a few quick shakes before dumping the pasta into the pan with the lamb. He turned off both burners on the stove and grabbed an oven mitt. When he removed the pan from the oven, the smell of hot, toasted garlic bread mixed with the delicious aroma of cooked onions and peppers already filling the kitchen. Putting the oven mitt aside, he grabbed one of the pieces of bread off the pan and dropped it on the cutting board, sucking his fingers into his mouth at the slight burn. He sliced the bread into long strips and arranged them on the plates Trevor mutely handed him.

Finally, Owen spooned the pasta onto the plates. There. He set everything on the card table. That didn't look half bad. Even

Trevor's bread looked like it would probably be edible, but that was true if you added enough butter and garlic to just about anything.

He turned, ready to be the one to critique *Trevor's* baking for once, but Trevor was just standing there gaping at him.

"Um." Owen scratched the back of his neck, suddenly self-conscious. The shabbiness of his apartment suddenly flooded back to him, and surely someone as well-dressed as Trevor wasn't going to be impressed by something as easy as pasta and meat sauce. "I don't know what goes with pasta. Wine? I don't have that, but I have some beers in the fridge?"

"A beer would be great, thank you."

"Great. Beers all around. Go sit." Owen grabbed a couple of beers, as well as knives and forks and some paper towels to use as napkins. He hoped the actions covered his nervousness. Trevor sat in his original seat and Owen set everything on the table before dragging his chair back to the opposite side so they'd both have room to eat.

He took a few bites. Not bad. The veggies had been dropped off before he'd passed out this morning, so they were still crisp and the onions and peppers hadn't had too much time in the pan to overwhelm the natural sweetness of the tomatoes or the rich flavor of the meat. He glanced up sheepishly at Trevor. He was used to Trevor's criticisms of his baking, and brushed them off completely, because he *knew* how good he was at that. But this was different. Trevor had his eyes closed as he chewed slowly, but he always did that, it didn't mean anything.

"How is it?"

Trevor slowly opened his eyes. Owen's heart leapt in his chest at the look in those beautiful green eyes, and he ruthlessly squashed down those feelings he was determined not to think about.

"It's good."

"Yeah?"

"Yeah."

Owen ducked his head and went back to eating. Damn. A "good" from Trevor was worth more than any line around the block or fancy reviewer's praise any day.

"Of course, the garlic bread is the best part."

Owen couldn't help the laugh that escaped him. Trevor grinned back, and Owen felt something warm settle between them.

"Can I ask you a question?" Trevor asked, scooping up another bite.

"Will you anyway if I say no?"

"I was just wondering where you trained?"

"You mean, what gym?"

"No, no." Trevor grinned. "I mean *trained*. What culinary school did you go to? From your croissants I was guessing C.I. or L'Academie, but now with the lamb I don't know."

"Oh." Owen took a few more bites of pasta. It really was pretty good. "I didn't."

"You didn't…?"

"I didn't go. To cooking school," Owen clarified. "I mean, not unless you count working in a prison kitchen."

And oh, fuck. He really shouldn't have said that. He could kiss Trevor ever coming around again goodbye. Certainly not at times when he'd be alone with Owen. He'd probably try to warn Yvonne off too, but at least she already knew. Owen braced himself for the I'm-totally-not-judging-you-because-you-paid-your-debt-to-society-but-I-have-somewhere-else-important-to-be face that most people made when learning

Owen was an ex-con, followed by a hasty retreat. He looked up at Trevor.

Trevor didn't have that look on his face. He looked more like… Well, he looked more like he'd been hit with a frying pan, honestly.

"You're self-trained?"

"Uh yeah, I guess," Owen said, confused. This was not the reaction he'd been expecting.

"You're self-trained! Of course, you are." Trevor looked to the ceiling like he was telling all this to God, not Owen. "This explains so much. You have no idea. No idea at all."

Trevor put his face in his hands and was quiet for a minute before letting out the sigh of a man who'd skipped past all the stages of grief and gone straight to acceptance. "No wonder your ordering system was such a mess."

His head snapped up, a delighted gleam in his eyes. "And why you were calling the beignets, 'big-nets'!"

"Hey!" said Owen. He tried to sound affronted, but it was hard in the face of Trevor's obvious glee. "That's what my nana called them. You can blame her, she's the one who taught me. And she'd kick your ass if she heard you making fun of her pronunciation."

With a laugh, Trevor reached for his beer. "She sounds amazing. Tell me about her."

Owen sobered, he could tell Trevor the short, sanitary version, but Trevor hadn't even batted an eye about the prison thing, and had been unexpectedly decent about Owen's scars. But no one who heard the full story ever ended up sticking around for long, and he wanted him around as long as possible. Still, Trevor was smart, if he stayed around Owen long enough he'd figure it out. It wasn't like the truth was further away than a quick Google search of his name anyway. Maybe it was best to just tell him now, when it would hurt less to lose him.

Owen's heart clenched at the thought. He didn't think it would ever hurt less to lose Trevor, not now, not even as friends or whatever they were, but he deserved the truth. All of it.

Owen finished the last of his beer and grabbed another before sitting back down. He sure as hell wasn't going to do this sober.

"Owen?" Trevor seemed to have sensed the change in his mood. "You don't have to tell me anything. I understand that family can be—"

"My parents dropped out of my life as soon as I was born," Owen interrupted. He looked down at his beer. He might be able to say this, but he didn't think he could look at Trevor while he did it. "I don't know if they're dead or in jail and I've never bothered to find out. I was bounced around the family for a while, but when I was thirteen I saw a guy run into a convenience store but leave his car running. I was a scrawny little thing back then, could barely see over the dashboard. When I crashed into the pawn shop, they said it was intentional, that I meant to rob the place."

He shrugged. "So, I went to juvie for a while. Got out when I was sixteen. Too young to legally be on my own, but no one in my family would take me back. Except Nana. Never went to church a day in her life, but the woman had the heart of the saint and the vocabulary of a Marine. She thought the baking would keep me out of trouble. 'Idle hands' and all."

Owen took another long drink, finishing the bottle. "But it didn't. Fell in with a bad crowd, was in and out of prison most my life. She always took me in when I needed a place to stay though, and taught me everything she knew."

He'd never told anyone else this last part. "One night, I was driving back to the chop shop I was working at when blue flashing lights came on in the rearview mirror. Next thing I knew, I was going eighty in a fifty-five in a car that wasn't mine with three cop cars chasing me. Went around a corner on two wheels and suddenly had a choice to run into a motorcyclist or a ditch.

"I chose the ditch. Woke up handcuffed to a hospital bed and decided that when I got out of prison, I wasn't going back. Four years in, I get a letter from some aunt. Turns out Nana was crossing the street to buy a pack of smokes, slipped on some ice, and that was it."

Owen laughed wetly. "Always said those damn things would kill her. She'd been there for me all my life and in the end…"

He sat there, hands picking at the label on his beer. "I got paroled a couple months later. She left me everything. Wasn't much, but it was enough to open Nana O'Neill's."

Owen never talked this much, but now that he'd started, he couldn't seem to stop. "She'd always wanted to open her own place someday, but it never happened. Life, and kids, and then fuckup grandkids, y'know? So I named the place after her and make all of her recipes.

"And that's my story," he finished softly.

There. He'd said it. All of it. He felt lighter, as if even if Trevor didn't like what he'd heard, it would be okay. Just the act of saying the words was freeing. An absolution almost. Like by telling someone about his nana, she lived on, just a little bit. It didn't make being alone much easier to bear though.

He picked up his plate and silverware, and took them to the

sink to rinse. The noise of the sink filling with running water was the only sound in the apartment.

"She sounds like an amazing woman."

Owen jumped. He hadn't even heard Trevor move, but here he was, standing next to him, holding his plate out.

"She was," Owen said, taking the plate and dunking it into the soap suds. Then he gathered up the rest of the pots and pans and started scrubbing. Trevor picked up a dish towel and dried the clean plates as Owen handed them to him.

"I never knew my grandmothers," Trevor said. Owen looked over at him out of the corner of his eye, but Trevor was staring at the knife he was drying. "They both died before I was born. Only child, parents are divorced, my mother's in Florida, my father's an asshole. Wanted me to turn out just like him. Sometimes I worry I have."

He put the knife carefully aside and started drying the colander. "He's a hateful, vicious, *little* man. He's a crook—the legal kind with hedge funds."

Trevor flashed a quick look over at him, but before Owen could respond, he continued. "I took just enough business classes all through college to get him to keep paying tuition, but I can't tell you how disappointed he was to end up with a son with a liberal arts degree instead. Luckily, I fell into a job I love and never looked back.

"I haven't spoken to my father since the day I graduated. Every time I say something cruel, I don't know if I hear it in his voice or my own, but I don't know how to stop. And that's *my* story."

Owen put down the pan he'd been washing. Trevor was watching him now, waiting for a response just as Owen had waited for his, with the silent knowledge that what had just been said might change everything. And maybe waiting for some of that same absolution too.

Owen didn't think, just reached out, framing Trevor's face in his soapy hands and kissed him.

Trevor responded immediately, both his hands coming up to grab Owen's shirt and drag him in even closer. He made a soft little "huh" noise as he opened his mouth to deepen the kiss.

Owen took full advantage, pressing in with a growl. He wanted to devour Trevor, to taste every inch of him and take him apart piece by piece to see what made him tick, but this wasn't the time. He reined himself in, instead licking carefully into Trevor's mouth, thrilling at the way the light caresses made him squirm and at the full body shudder he got when he lapped at the roof of Trevor's mouth.

Trevor gave as good as he got, pressing his full length against Owen with slow, tortuous rolls of his hips. Owen turned them, pulling Trevor with him until Owen was leaning back against the kitchen counter, legs spread enough for Trevor to stand between them. For this, he was rewarded by Trevor slanting his full body weight against him, only to pull back with a hiss as their hard cocks rubbed against each other through the soft layers of clothing. Trevor immediately dove back in, peppering Owen's mouth with infuriating little bites, but never holding still long enough to let Owen get a good taste.

Owen dropped a hand from Trevor's face and grabbed his ass instead. The swell of muscle fit perfectly into his hand and Trevor moaned as he squeezed again. Owen reluctantly let go and ran his hand up Trevor's back under his shirt. Under *Owen's* shirt. He growled again as that thought pushed him even closer to the edge. The soft rub of fabric against his dick as Trevor continued to rhythmically thrust against him didn't help either. At this rate, he'd come in his pants like a damn teenager.

Owen had just enough time to enjoy the warm skin between Trevor's shoulder blades, before Trevor was pulling away.

"Stop, I can't," he said, breathing hard.

"Sure you can." Owen tried to reel him back in for another kiss, but Trevor pushed him back, both hands against his chest. His eyes were still closed, like they were every time he sampled the things Owen offered him.

"Trev," Owen said, hearing the pathetic desperation in his own voice. But Trevor backed away out of his reach, leaving him alone and confused.

"No, Owen, I can't. And I—I can't tell you why."

Owen felt his heart stutter and grow cold. "Oh, you can't, huh? You got some big secret you can't share? Tell me, is it something worse than almost running down an innocent person or spending years in jail? Because I told you all about that."

"No," Trevor said, so quietly Owen could barely hear him. "I just don't want you to hate me."

Owen felt all his anger leave in a rush. Fuck.

"I'm not going to hate you, Trev. Whatever it is, you don't owe me anything. I understand."

And he did. Just because Owen couldn't keep his hands and emotions to himself, that wasn't Trevor's fault. He was under no obligation to return Owen's feelings and Owen sure as shit wasn't going to guilt him into something he didn't want. Sure, he's hoped for a fairy tale ending, true love's first kiss and all that. But guys like him didn't get a happily ever after.

"I think I'd better go," Trevor whispered.

"Yeah. I think so too."

Owen stayed leaning against the counter as Trevor collected his things. Right before he disappeared out of sight down the stairs, Owen couldn't stop himself.

"Hey, Trev?"

"Yeah?" Trevor looked back at him through the gaps in the handrail.

"I'll see you around?"

"Yeah." Trevor smiled sadly, then continued down the stairs until he was out of sight.

Owen waited for the sound of the door opening and closing, then Trevor's car driving away. He brought his hands up to cover his face and let out a deep, heartfelt curse. Of course he couldn't have just been happy with a good thing, he always had to push it. Every. Single. Time. And where did that always get him? Right back where he started.

Alone.

CHAPTER 13

That night, all alone in his big, cold bed in his big, cold condo, Trevor couldn't sleep. Fuck, he was an asshole. He rolled over and tried to get comfortable on his goose-down pillows and thousand thread-count sheets. His memory foam mattress didn't feel nearly as soft as that old sofa in Owen's apartment had when he'd sat on it to fold Owen's clothes. Clothes like Owen's shirt that he'd "borrowed" and was now wearing in bed.

He groaned and rolled onto his back.

Jesus Christ, Hill, obvious much? And what were you even thinking? That was some serious stalker shit, going through his apartment while he was asleep and folding his clothes. You're lucky Owen kissed you instead of punching you in the face.

He groaned again, this time for an entirely different reason. That *kiss*. A man would do terrible, terrible things to be kissed like that. He ran his fingers over his lips. All that heat and power under his hands, his lips, his entire body—and he'd pushed Owen away.

Trevor dropped his hand with a sigh. Why had he done that? It wasn't like Owen would be the first chef he ever fucked who didn't know Trevor was a food critic. Hell, he'd even given Owen a good review, *two* good reviews, beforehand. So why did he feel so guilty? It wasn't like there was any difference between sleeping with Owen after lying to him for months than there was with anyone else.

Just keep telling yourself that.

Trevor rolled over, still unable to get comfortable. He knew the real reason. It was the same reason he'd folded Owen's damn socks, and done his paperwork, and kept showing up at the bakery door like a dog begging for scraps of attention. The same reason he'd told Owen about his father, and being a disappointment, and why he wanted desperately to tell Owen everything, to let him know that Trevor was a caustic, two-faced critic who was hated by everyone in Owen's profession and who would one day turn that vitriol on him as well, just for a few moments of his readers' amusement.

It was the same reason Owen's life story didn't repel him the way Owen had so clearly expected, but only made Trevor love him more.

Trevor pulled the blankets over his head in a vain attempt to block out the word.

Love.

He'd never felt anything like this before, but knew that's what it was. He loved Owen, was *in love* with him and couldn't bear the idea that Owen had told him everything, had told him his deepest, darkest secrets, and Trevor couldn't even bear to tell him his own job. Owen deserved better and that was the reason Trevor had pushed him away.

But he knew himself too well to believe he'd be able to stay away forever. He was far too selfish and greedy. He still wanted Owen more than anything, even if he knew that—for Owen's own good—he couldn't have him. So, if he couldn't stay away and Owen deserved better, then Trevor was just going to have to redouble his self-control. If he could've controlled himself better from the beginning and just been happy with a good thing, he wouldn't be in this mess.

Of course, if he'd controlled himself better he'd never have gotten the chance to know how surprisingly soft Owen's stubble was, or the rumbling, satisfied noises he made when Trevor fell against him, but that didn't bear thinking about.

No more spending all day in the kitchen with Owen, laughing with him and working on the books. Owen didn't need him for that any longer since Trevor had explained it and the accounting software would make it much easier. No more secret parking space and special entrance. Trevor would use the front door and wait in line like any other customer. If he happened to see Owen, great, and if not, there was always the next time he came in. Or the next. Or...

Trevor nodded to himself in resolve, then sighed like the pathetic idiot he was. This was going to hurt.

He curled up in a corner of the bed. He'd take some time to wallow before heading back to Nana O'Neill's. He was smart enough to recognize his pattern of avoidance, but one personal problem at a time.

※ ※ ※

To his credit, Trevor managed to stay away from the bakery for three whole days.

He came by on a midday lull so he wouldn't have to stand in line for an hour, but when he saw Yvonne's face he wished it'd taken longer. Maybe then he'd know what to say to her.

"Just a cinnamon roll. No coffee." He tried to act confident and bored, like this was just his normal routine with a regular acquaintance and not someone he'd jokingly called "Dr. Jekyll" for an entire week after she'd told him about her thesis until

Owen punched him in the arm and told him to quit harassing the staff. From the look on her face, he was about to meet Ms. Hyde.

He broke almost instantly. "Please?"

She still didn't move and the woman in line behind Trevor coughed pointedly. Yvonne glared at her.

"Wait your turn."

She then turned the full force of that glare on Trevor. Years of having Rachel as his boss meant Trevor was used to having terrifying women pissed at him, but he was still petrified at the daggers in her eyes.

"You are one stupid motherfucker, you know that?" she said.

The woman in line behind him gasped but Trevor didn't have time to say anything before Yvonne continued. "I am going to say this very slowly, but I am only going to say this once, so you'd better listen. Owen is my friend—"

"Just *friends*?" Trevor quipped, because yes, he'd figured that out about the same time Owen's hands were getting intimately acquainted with his ass, but still. Trevor Hill: Professional Dickhead.

"No," Yvonne continued slowly. "Not 'just' anything. He is my friend. He's the kindest, most protective man I know. When I first realized I was attracted to girls as well as guys, he was the first person I told because I knew he'd make me feel safe. But he takes care of everyone *except* himself. Which means that as his friend, I have to be the one to look out for him. If you keep hurting him the way you've been hurting him, I'll rip your balls off and feed them to you. Understood?"

Trevor nodded. He was doing all this just so he *wouldn't* hurt Owen.

She stared at him for longer than he was comfortable with, then shook her head. She grabbed the last cinnamon roll out of the display. "That'll be $5.16."

Trevor didn't say anything at being charged the "foodie" price, just handed her a ten and turned to leave before she could offer him his change.

"Hey, Trevor?" she called out as he reached the door. "For what it's worth, I don't think you and Owen are friends..."

Trevor's heart sank. "I'm starting to get that, thanks."

He was halfway down the block before she could respond.

CHAPTER 14

Owen hummed thoughtfully as he carefully turned the miniature cups, each containing their own personal-sized apple cobbler. They looked okay, and smelled pretty damn delicious, but Owen had always been partial to apple and cinnamon, so what did he know?

He grabbed a fork out of one of the drawers and eyed the least-attractive cobbler warily. It *should* taste good, it was still the same basic recipe as his nana's apple pie filling, and tweaking the snickerdoodle recipe to make the topping made sense, but he'd never tried to create something of his own before and he was nervous.

It was part of why he hated those damn Mr. Tasty reviews. The man made him sound like some sort of baking genius, but Owen wasn't a genius, he was just good at following directions. Anybody could do that. About the most adventurous he'd ever gotten was adding that creme de menthe to the chocolate mousse, but mint and chocolate? That was obvious.

His traitorous mind brought up the memory of Trevor looking up at him while licking chocolate off his lips. He scowled and grabbed a mixing bowl.

Okay sure, he might have *adjusted* a couple of things, like changing from store-bought Red Delicious apples to those locally grown Braeburn apples when he'd learned that there even *was* more than one kind of apple. Or when he'd adjusted the cook times when he started selling more reasonable portions. Or when he'd tweaked the new motor on the mixer to go faster so that his meringues could be even lighter. But that was just practical stuff. It didn't make him some kind of pastry chef. If the recipe said apple pie, he ended up with an apple pie, and it was his nana's apple pie so it had to be good.

But not this time. This time Owen had ended up with something different, made it into his *own* recipe, and he had no idea if it was even sellable.

He cut into the cobbler with the fork and was pleased to see a little steam escape, releasing the scent of nutmeg into the air. That was a new addition to the recipe too. Nana only ever used cinnamon, but he always thought nutmeg brought extra warmth to a recipe, and he was pretty sure he'd added just the right amount of cloves to ground the flavor too.

Looks okay. He examined the small bite on his fork before cautiously popping it into his mouth.

It tasted... good? At least there wasn't anything obviously wrong with it. He'd never been that great of a judge of his own cooking anyway. Sure, he knew he was pretty alright—he'd never have sunk everything into opening his own bakery if he didn't—but he had no idea what that Mr. Tasty guy was talking about when he said things like "a cascade of decadence" or "a hedonistic explosion of pleasure". Not if he was talking about food anyway.

And then there were Trevor's criticisms, which, sure, he was a dick about, but were sometimes actually useful.

"Try this." Owen said, turning around with another bite on the fork, his other hand cupped underneath to catch it if it fell. He looked over at the counter where Trevor always worked and... Right.

Owen snarled and tossed the bite in the sink. He grabbed a clean fork and the rest of the cobbler and carried them out front. He took a quick glance around the tables in the bakery. No reason, just to see who was there. He certainly wasn't looking for any smart-mouthed, long-legged figure in particular.

"Need a second opinion," he grunted, and thrust the cobbler at Yvonne. She ignored him long enough to finish selling some kid in a waistcoat a six-pack of lamingtons, then turned to him. He didn't like how quickly her look of exasperation turned to one of understanding and pity.

"How's it taste?" he asked.

She took a bite, then another. "It's delicious," she said, scooping more into her mouth.

He reached out to take the rest of the sample away now that she'd given her review, but she hissed at him and clutched it closer.

"Back off, it's mine."

"Good enough to sell then?"

She rolled her eyes. If she wasn't careful, her face was gonna stick that way.

She handed him back the fork and ran a finger around the inside of the cup to get the last bits of cobbler. "Yes, Owen, they're good enough to sell. Now bring the rest of them out here and get back to work, we're almost out of biscotti."

Owen carried the fork back into the kitchen, grumbling. He hated biscotti. They reminded him of those fake bricks they used in construction to make it look like people had brick walls when they didn't. Ever since he'd bought that damned espresso machine though, they'd been selling like hotcakes.

He looked again at the empty spot where Trevor used to sit.

Honestly, he was kind of pissed. Sure, maybe that kiss didn't end the way he'd hoped, but at least he'd been a goddamn adult about it. He'd only sulked a little, and even then, Yvonne was the only one who'd caught him at it. He hadn't pressed Trevor on it, or mentioned it at all when he saw him.

Which was getting to be less and less often. Sure, Trevor still came into the bakery, but he hadn't used the back door or even come into the kitchen once since then. He just acted like any other damn regular waiting in line to get their daily coffee and treat.

Or weekly coffee and treat.

Owen grabbed a set of measuring spoons and threw them on the counter. He was madder at himself than anyone else. He'd used the money Trevor's help had saved him to buy that damn espresso machine just because he'd always harped on about the coffee. Owen figured that might get some sort of wry remark out of him at least, but no, instead Trevor came by even less often than before.

He'd even hired a new kid to run the damn thing. Turned out he was some kind of hotshot coffee genius who'd heard about Nana O'Neill's and had actually begged Owen for the job. He'd been willing to help out with the daily cleaning as well in exchange for total freedom over the coffee menu and permission to share his drinks with his zillions of followers on Twitter or TikTok or Insta-whatever. That last part worried Owen a little, but Yvonne seemed to get along with him and he trusted her judgment more than his own. But the word that Nana O'Neill's now had the best coffee in town just meant longer lines, and longer lines meant even less Trevor.

And even more damn biscotti.

Owen walked over to the fridge and pulled out the eggs,

butter, and a container of pre-zested lemon. That was another change he'd made in the months since their kiss. He'd taken Trevor's suggestion about getting some help and called the Grand River Community College. Turns out their culinary program had several students who'd be thrilled to come in at the asscrack of dawn to do the prep work. He probably could have gotten more advanced help from some Culinary Institute kids, but the GRCC felt right.

He'd even mentioned this to Trevor one of the times he'd seen him, dropping hints about how more help would mean Owen could sleep in most days and have more free time. But Trevor had just said, "That's great" before paying for his food and finding a seat at the furthest table from the kitchen.

That was the last time Owen had seen him and alright, fine. He could take a hint. But even just as a *friend* he thought Trevor would appreciate that Owen had taken his suggestions, even when they seemed like a risk or just added to the headache. Before, Owen just had a quiet little bakery and one employee. Now he had a staff, and a waiting list of kids who wanted to get the chance to learn from *him*.

But no. Trevor couldn't handle a little bit of awkwardness. Fine. Whatever, fuck Trevor. He was probably getting his pastries somewhere else too. Not that Owen was jealous.

He put his hands on the counter and took a deep breath. Anger might help with kneading bread, but it was only going to make him fuck up the biscotti. He looked up at the clock on the opposite wall to time his breaths, *One, two, three in. One, two, three out.* But his eye caught on the two frames under it. Yvonne had gotten Mr. Tasty's reviews professionally framed and hung them up in the kitchen, telling Owen he should be proud of his achievements.

You know what? Fuck Mr. Tasty too. He wanted to call Owen an "old-school homestyle baker mastering all the traditional classics"? Owen would show him "old-school."

He pushed the biscotti ingredients aside next to the forgotten apple cobblers. If Mr. Tasty thought he was so great, let's see what he said when Owen *didn't* do what he was supposed to. He'd started Nana O'Neill's just baking what he wanted, when he wanted. And he didn't want to make any more damn biscotti or the same old recipes he'd made a thousand times.

Filled with this new determination, he stalked back over to the refrigerator and this time pulled out the chilled phyllo dough he'd shown the kids how to make that morning, just like his nana had shown him.

He was going to make those damn mini-baklavas he'd been thinking about, and he was going to make them using no one's recipe but his own. Hell, maybe he'd even make some kind of fancy garnish for them too. So what if you weren't supposed to decorate baklava? If it wasn't "traditional"? Owen was gonna make something that looked and tasted the way *he* thought it should.

And if Trevor, or Mr. Tasty, or every single customer he had didn't like it, that was their problem.

CHAPTER 15

Trevor carefully looked around the edge of his newspaper while the barista filmed the process of making Trevor's coffee with his phone. He felt ridiculous, like a spy in a terrible movie. He lowered the paper.

He saw the guy frown as he read the name Yvonne had written on the cup, and stood, making sure to lay his newspaper and half eaten torte down in such a way that suggested, "This table is taken. Don't even think about it."

"Uh, 'Moron'?" the guy called out uncertainly. "I have a triple dark cherry macchiato for 'Moron'?"

"That's me," Trevor said, swiping the coffee from his hand. He glared at Yvonne, but she didn't deign to look his way.

Trevor took a sip as he returned to his table. Christ, that was good. Not as good as the pear and hazelnut chocolate torte he'd gotten to go with it, of course. If he knew Nana had recipes like that up her sleeve, he would've begged Owen to make them for him months ago. Actually begged.

He tried to push the thoughts of other ways he could have tried to convince Owen out of his mind. That right there was exactly why he'd had to step back and stop acting like he deserved to be in the kitchen with Owen. And when just visiting Nana O'Neill's as a regular customer every day had turned out to be too much of a temptation, he'd limited himself to these weekly visits. Visits that he looked forward to from the second he walked out the door the week before.

He knew he was pathetic, but he couldn't help it. It just felt so right for him to be at Nana O'Neill's and he'd learned if he took his time drinking his coffee, he had a better chance of catching a glimpse of Owen from behind his newspaper, even though Owen rarely seemed to come to the front of the shop anymore.

He was broken from his melancholy with the loud crack of a plate slamming onto the table next to his last few bites of torte. Trevor startled, nearly spilling his coffee, and looked up to see who'd dropped the plate.

It was Owen. Trevor drank in the sight of him. He had his arms crossed over a sleeveless shirt that did little to hide either his scars or his tattoos. His apron was tossed over one shoulder and a smear of sugar-y something glittered on his cheek. From this angle he looked *good*. He looked big. He looked hot.

He looked pissed.

Trevor opened his mouth, not sure what he was going to say, but Owen spoke before he even had the chance.

"Eat this."

Gladly, but in front of all these customers?

Thankfully, Trevor's brain-to-mouth filter was turned on for once, and he dragged his eyes away from Owen to the plate in front of him. It still rocked slightly back and forth from the impact. On it sat two pastries that Trevor couldn't immediately identify. They were round, but slightly lumpy and coated with a light glaze. They were still hot too, steam wafting up from them, but didn't look baked, more like they had just been pulled fresh from the fryer. The *new* fryer Owen had bought to go along with the new coffee machine, new staff, and all the other improvements he'd made without Trevor's help. Trevor was so goddamn proud of him and his success.

The glaze on the pastries was melting from the heat, dripping slowly from the sides. Trevor breathed in, and was hit with the mouthwatering aroma of fried dough, berries, and the first rays of summer sun.

"What is it?"

"Goddamn hipster food is what it is," Owen said with a sneer. "I took my croissant recipe and figured out a way to fry it like a donut. I hear that's popular."

It took Trevor a minute to clear the saliva from his mouth before he could speak.

"You made *cronuts*?" he whispered hoarsely.

"Naw," Owen picked one of the pastries off the plate and tore a chunk off. The bright scent of lemon hit Trevor along with a whiff of something floral he couldn't identify. Owen popped the chunk into his mouth and chewed thoughtfully.

"I thought I'd try something new. I tweaked the recipe for lemon curd and folded that into the croissant dough with some blueberries so they're more like fritters. There's lavender in the glaze because I saw some at the market and figured, why not? Took a couple tries, but I think they turned out okay." Owen talked while he ate. Trevor wished he could be disgusted by the sight and not desperately turned on.

"If I put them on the menu, I'm going to call them 'critters'." Owen smiled before taking another bite and nudging the plate closer to Trevor. "Go on. Tell me what's wrong with 'em."

The sight of Owen's smile hit Trevor in the gut and stole his breath. He knew he'd missed Owen, but at that moment he honestly had no idea how he'd managed without seeing him every day. Not happily, that was for certain. Trevor smiled back, just the smallest bit, then without breaking eye contact, picked up the closest pastry—*Critters. What an enormous dork*—and took a bite.

Oh. *Oh.*

Trevor's eyes fluttered shut and he couldn't help the frankly obscene noise that escaped him. He thought he was used to Owen's amazing skills. Or at least acclimated enough to keep from embarrassing himself in public. But the way the fried dough melted in his mouth leading effortlessly to the sweet kiss of lavender glaze before dissolving again into the bite of tart lemon and rapturous burst of blueberry left him almost shaking in his chair.

"What do you think? Tell me the truth."

Trevor blinked his eyes open. The truth?

The truth was, this was the single greatest thing he'd ever eaten. Bar none.

The truth was, it made him feel warm to the very center of his core and melted away every fear or doubt that he'd ever had.

The truth was, he wanted to live with this feeling for the rest of his life.

The truth was, he would give it all up in a heartbeat in exchange for just one of the proud, shy smiles Owen was giving him now.

The truth was...

"I'm Mr. Tasty."

Owen's smile morphed into a look of confusion. Trevor didn't even notice, too intent on getting more of the critter in his mouth. He groaned again around another huge bite. This one had even more of the lemon curd than the first, and Trevor could die happy in that moment. There was a hint of nutmeg. He loved nutmeg.

"You're what?" Owen asked, uncertainty filling his voice.

"I'm Mr. Tasty," Trevor mumbled around the food in his mouth, blissed beyond all cares. What had he even been worried about? Telling Owen the truth felt *amazing*.

He continued, "You know, that guy you hate? The one every chef in the city hates? God, Owen, I'm sure you hate me even more now but I wasn't trying to lie to you or dig up dirt or anything. I just couldn't stay away and then it got to be too much because I wanted you. I wanted you so much but I couldn't lie to you, so I tried to stay away but that was even worse."

He swallowed the last bite of pastry down, and let its warmth give him the courage to finish. "I know I said shitty things to you about your food, but it's so good. It's so breathtakingly good, so I said it in my reviews instead. And I meant what I said there. I love your food, I love your bakery, and I'm pretty sure I love y—"

Owen swooped down and shut Trevor up with a kiss.

Oh, yes. Yes, this. It was even better than Trevor remembered. He made a needy noise and grabbed at Owen, desperate not to let him get away this time.

Owen opened Trevor up with his tongue and started to lick the taste of the pastry out of his mouth. Trevor tried to protest, but then he realized that Owen tasted like pastry too.

Mmm, delicious.

The kiss was so good, Trevor could hear a roaring in his ears, and he just wanted more and more, until suddenly he was wet and cold.

Trevor pulled back with a gasp. Oh. The roar had been the rest of the patrons in the bakery cheering and wolf whistling. Trevor immediately flushed with embarrassment. And the wet and cold had been?

"If you're quite finished," Yvonne said from where she was standing next to Owen, one foot tapping impatiently and an empty water pitcher in her hand.

Trevor flushed even redder. He hadn't been caught making out in public like that since he was a kid. He turned to look at Owen, mortified.

Owen, who was grinning like a loon at him. His white shirt was soaked through, showing his tattoos in a blur of colors through the translucent fabric and he had droplets of water caught in his eyelashes. Oh no, Yvonne had really not thought this through at all.

Owen's grin turned wolfish, and he grabbed Trevor again for a quick press of lips. He then took Trevor's hands and pulled him to his feet.

"Yvonne," he said as he backed toward the kitchen, bringing Trevor along with him. "I think we'd better close early today."

"Dammit, Owen. You can't just keep closing whenever you want. I don't care if you two did finally pull your heads out of your asses, it's called business sense. Trevor, tell him."

"You're right, Yvonne," Trevor said, not taking his eyes off Owen. "It's terrible business sense to base your store hours around a single person's availability. Yvonne, *you* should definitely stay open. *Owen and I* will be upstairs in his apartment however, and I'm sure sound travels…"

Owen's eyes darkened and he yanked Trevor in with a huff. Trevor laughed, and pushed him into the kitchen, before following him in for a kiss.

They broke apart just in time to hear Yvonne's, "You heard the man. Bakery's closed," followed by a disappointed "Awwww," that Trevor was pretty sure came from the knitting circle of old ladies in the corner.

"Mmm, no sex in the kitchen, Trev. Unsanitary. Get the health inspector on my ass."

Trevor groped the ass in question. "Better take me upstairs then. No health inspector's getting this, it's *mine*."

Owen all but shoved Trevor out the back door, grabbing the keys from the hook at the last moment. As the door swung closed behind them, Trevor caught Yvonne's voice drifting out saying, "...and if I hear one peep about Mr. Tasty's secret identity being discovered, I will ban every single..."

They finally got upstairs to Owen's apartment, but Trevor barely had time to catch his breath before Owen was spinning him around and pinning him against the wall.

"I'm still mad at you," Owen murmured, peppering bites down the side of Trevor's neck.

"Okay, great. Yes, mad. Mmm, right there..."

He whined as Owen pulled back.

"I'm serious."

Trevor sobered. "I know and I really am sorry. I shouldn't have run away. No, more than that, I should have trusted you enough to tell you, but I will do everything I can to make it up to you, I swear."

"Will you now?" Owen leaned in, lips brushing the delicate skin under Trevor's ear with every word. "Because I have to tell you, Trev. That might take a while, I'm really, really mad."

He rocked his hips. Trevor forgot how to breathe for a moment. Then Owen was back at work on his neck. Trevor moaned; the man was hell on his concentration.

"Can you be mad at me in a bed?" he finally panted. "Because I'm too old to do this against the wall."

Trevor caught Owen's muttered, "Next time," before he was

being pulled again, this time down the hall and into Owen's bedroom.

Trevor didn't have a chance to notice any of the features of the bedroom, nor did he particularly care, before he was being tossed down onto the king-size bed in the middle of the room. Literally, picked up and *tossed*. He didn't think he had a thing for being manhandled before, but apparently he'd been wrong. *Very* wrong.

He sat up and unbuttoned his wet shirt. "This is a silk blend. I'm going to mention the terrible staff in my next review."

He threw it to the side and started to work on his belt, but at the lack of response he looked up. Owen was standing at the foot of the bed watching him.

"What?"

"Nothin'," Owen said, shaking his head. "Just enjoying the show."

Trevor rolled his eyes. "Come here."

Owen crawled onto the bed and settled on Trevor's lap, facing him with one thick thigh either side of Trevor's legs. Trevor wrapped his arms low around Owen's back to hold him in place. It wasn't like he'd actually be able to keep Owen there if he didn't want to be, he might as well try to hold onto a hurricane, but the man seemed content where he was. He draped his heavy arms over Trevor's shoulders and smiled down at him.

"Hey, there."

"Hey, yourself. Planning to get this show on the road anytime soon?"

"Mmm, not sure." Owen cupped his hands around the back of Trevor's neck and started kneading the muscles there.

Trevor hissed. Oh fuck, that felt good. Owen chuckled and moved his hands to Trevor's bare shoulders. He started kneading again, this time with even more force, and Trevor dissolved. He'd never expected to be jealous of bread, but if this was how Owen handled the dough every day?

Trevor sobbed and dug his fingers into Owen's shirt as Owen hit a particularly sore knot. Owen continued to work the spot, and the next thing Trevor knew, he was breathing in the cotton of Owen's damp shirt, Owen's solid form the only thing holding him vaguely upright. Had he been drooling? How mortifying. He opened eyes that he didn't remember closing. Right, the shirt was damp from Yvonne's impromptu wet t-shirt contest. He fisted his hands in the material at Owen's back, pulling the translucent shirt tight across his chest. *Very* nice. He'd have to get Yvonne a thank you card. Or maybe a thank you Porsche. Or maybe the phone number for a lovely redhead he knew—he owed Rachel a favor anyway.

All thoughts of his friend fled as Owen's hands let up from the kneading motion and started brushing down Trevor's back, sweeping away all the tension in his entire body. At Trevor's groan, Owen's hips jerked against his, and apparently there was one part of Trevor's anatomy still capable of being upright. He snickered.

"Something funny?" Owen asked, pulling Trevor tighter against him and rubbing circles into Trevor's back with his large, warm hands.

"Mmm, keep doing that," Trevor mumbled into his chest.

"Thought you wanted to get this show on the road?"

Trevor sighed. Sex or massage? Sex or massage? Why did he have to make all the hard decisions? He lazed against Owen, still deciding, until Owen brought one hand around and slid it into Trevor's open fly.

Sex. Yes, definitely. Definitely sex.

Trevor squirmed and plucked at Owen's shirt.

"Off. Off, off, off..."

Owen laughed and pushed him gently back. Trevor huffed as he fell against the pillows, but before he could complain, Owen was stripping his shirt off with both hands. The ability to speak left Trevor entirely, and he made a hungry sound.

Shirtless, sleepy Owen in a towel was one thing—one beautiful, glorious thing—but shirtless, horny Owen, towering over Trevor and holding his hips down with his body weight? That was the kind of thing that could make a man weep. Or spontaneously combust. Honestly, Trevor was about fifty-fifty at the moment.

"This okay?" Owen asked, voice thick. "I can put it back on."

Why would Owen even suggest such a terrible thing? His eyes drifted across Owen's broad chest, trying to take in as much of it as he could, when he realized Owen was worried about his scars. There were a lot of them, standing out starkly against his tattooed skin, but they were a part of Owen, and Trevor wanted all of him.

"Don't you dare," he whispered. "Show me."

Watching Trevor through hooded eyes, Owen slowly unbuttoned his jeans and slid down his fly, inch by torturous inch. Tease. Trevor couldn't look away as Owen rose up on his knees and pushed his jeans and boxers down his hips to just under the swell of his ass. Owen's cock sprang free from the confining fabric and slapped up against his navel, leaving a smear of precome just below his belly button.

Trevor gave another inarticulate noise. He needed that. He needed that now. He struggled to sit up, but Owen pinned him effortlessly with one giant hand in the center of his chest. And apparently today was a day of firsts because Trevor was learning about all *sorts* of kinks he didn't know he had.

Owen rumbled out a laugh and started slowly stroking his cock with his free hand. He put on a show, moaning and throwing his head back as he slowly palmed the entire length. It was quite a length. Trevor might feel self-conscious if he was capable of thinking anything more than, *Want want want want want want.* He struggled against Owen just enough for show, and was rewarded by Owen pressing him even more firmly into the bed.

Owen grinned savagely and rocked his ass down against Trevor's still-clothed erection.

"Hmm," he said, rolling his hips again, making Trevor's eyes cross. Owen slid his hand up to the head of his cock and gently rubbed the precome there with his thumb. "So, how do you want to do this?"

Trevor choked and tried to grab at Owen, but could only reach his thighs, his nails scrabbling against the unforgiving denim. Owen ignored Trevor's plight and continued his leisurely stroking. His voice was like distant thunder.

"'Cause I was thinking that I wanted you to fuck me, but now that I've got you here, I think I wanna fuck you instead."

He tilted his head, considering, then nodded as if he'd decided. "Definitely wanna taste you though. Let's start there."

That was all the warning Trevor had, before Owen was abruptly off him. Owen moved to the bedside table and rummaged in it for a minute. Trevor raised his head to see what he was doing just in time to catch Owen's wink as Owen shimmied off his jeans and boxers before pulling Trevor's pants and underwear off in one smooth motion. Trevor didn't even have time to enjoy the sight of him fully naked before Owen dove in.

Trevor shouted, his entire body curling up as he was enveloped in warm, wet heat. Owen slid his body in between Trevor's legs, nudging his thighs until Trevor took the hint, and lifted his legs to drape one over each massive shoulder. Owen took Trevor as deep as he could for just a moment, before pulling back to press light kisses to the underside of Trevor's cock.

The kisses were somehow even more intimate than the rest of it, the light press of Owen's lips more than just the promise of a good, hard fuck, but of something more, something Trevor wasn't quite sure he could put a name to. But with Owen's help, it was something they could figure out together.

He heard the snick of a cap being opened, then one of Owen's thick fingers, slick with lube, was pressing against his entrance, not penetrating, just there.

"This okay?" Owen asked again, lips whispering against Trevor's overheated skin.

"Yeah," panted Trevor, hands twisting in the sheets. Owen pressed a quick kiss to his hipbone and Trevor felt a flush of warm affection for this man. This wonderful man, who looked so tough and whose life had been so hard, but who still retained such a sweet tenderness that was evident in everything from his baking to his lovemaking.

Then Owen bit down on the spot he'd just kissed, sucking hard and worrying the skin with his teeth and the flush of warmth Trevor felt suddenly turned into something much hotter.

"Fuck! In me. In me now, you fucker." Trevor kicked Owen's back with his foot. Owen looked up from the hickey he'd made and grinned. He pushed his finger into Trevor unhurriedly, and Trevor threw an arm over his eyes with a groan.

"I hate you so much."

"No, you don't," said Owen confidently. He pushed his finger all the way in and held it there, letting Trevor adjust.

"No, I don't." Trevor swore. He tried to twist his hips to get Owen's finger to move or get even deeper, but was stilled by Owen's other hand against his hip, holding him in place. "Fuck you."

"Next time," Owen said amicably. He moved his finger in and out a few times, still at that maddeningly glacial pace, then slid a second one in alongside it, the entire time licking over the mark he'd made.

"Really, Owen, a hickey?" Trevor asked when he'd gathered enough brain cells to speak. He kicked Owen's back again. "What, are you going to ask me to wear your letterman jacket next?"

"You do look good in my clothes," Owen agreed. "Look good with my mark on you too."

With that, he moved to lick the sensitive spot just under the head of Trevor's cock at the same time his fingers, three now, found that perfect place inside Trevor that made electric shocks shoot down his spine.

Trevor swore, then started shivering as his body was wracked with pleasure. Owen took the opportunity to get as much of Trevor in his mouth as possible. Trevor felt the head of his cock brush the soft palate of Owen's mouth, then slide further, all the way into his throat. Owen hummed in satisfaction and Trevor's hips bucked up uncontrollably.

Owen pulled off, coughing and resting his head on Trevor's hip while he caught his breath.

"Sorry! Sorry," said Trevor, running his hands soothingly over Owen's scalp.

Well done, Trevor. Way to kill the mood. Owen's short hair prickled against his palms, so he scratched lightly with his nails instead. In his lap, Owen just about started purring.

"S'okay," Owen slurred, voice rough. He stayed there a minute though, basking in Trevor's apologetic ministrations.

"Hey, get up here," Trevor said softly. He shuddered as Owen gently pulled his fingers out, body clutching at the emptiness. Then Owen was above him, elbows braced on either side of Trevor's head, looking down at him. Trevor leaned up for a kiss, and Owen met him halfway. He could taste himself on Owen's tongue, a sharp bitterness that had his cock, which had softened somewhat, roaring back to full hardness.

He ran his hands over Owen's arms up to his shoulders, enjoying the way the powerful muscles flexed as they held Owen's body over his own. Owen broke the kiss.

"You don't have to," he said to a spot just to the right of Trevor's ear.

"What?"

"You don't have to touch them," Owen said. "I know they're gross."

Trevor looked up at him quizzically, but Owen wouldn't look at him.

Gross? Gross was the absolute *last* word Trevor would use to describe any part of Owen. Brawny, funny, sarcastic, passionate, intense, hotter-than-hell, but gross?

He looked at his hands still clutched happily around Owen's biceps. Oh, the scars again.

Owen sighed and started to pull away.

Trevor felt a rush of rage at whoever made him feel this

way. He used his anger and Owen's distraction to roll them over, riding the momentum until he was on top. Owen's surprise gave him the second he needed to grasp both of his wrists and pin them above his head in one hand.

"Now you listen to *me*," Trevor said fiercely. He grasped Owen's chin with his free hand, forcing him to meet his eyes. Owen's eyes bugged out in shock, but he stayed silent.

"I want you, and that means all of you. I love your scars, not because I have to just because I love you, but because they are part of what *makes* you the man I love. They're a testament to your pain, your conscience, and how you work so hard to do the best you can with what you're given every single day. I don't want to just touch them, Owen, I want to *taste* them. I want to be able to draw them from memory the same as I want to know the story behind every single tattoo. I want to know them better than I know myself, just like I want to know every part of you. Is that clear?"

Owen nodded, dazed. He raised one of his hands in Trevor's grip, like a student waiting for permission to ask a question.

"Yes?"

"You love me?"

"Obviously," said Trevor with a bravado he didn't quite feel. He *did* love Owen, he was certain of it, but he wasn't exactly used to saying the words.

"Oh," Owen said. "Same."

"Yeah?" Trevor asked, ducking his chin in a vain attempt to cover his sudden blush.

"Yeah. I love you too, Trev."

"Good. I'm glad that's settled."

Owen rolled his eyes at him, and they stayed there a moment, just looking at each other, before Trevor remembered other, more pressing concerns. He cleared his throat.

"I'm going to ride your dick now, and you're just going to have to lie there and enjoy it."

Owen laughed and let out a fake sigh, relaxing back into the bed. "If I have to."

"You do."

Owen shrugged. "You do what you gotta do, Trev."

Trevor grinned, and ducked down for a quick kiss that turned into a much longer and dirtier one than he'd intended, before scooting back. Owen broke his hold effortlessly and reached out to fumble blindly with the same bedside drawer, before pulling out a condom and slapping it against Trevor's stomach.

Trevor slid it over Owen's cock as quickly as he could, knowing that if he lingered, he'd get distracted and not get what he really wanted. He squeezed a little bit more lube out and spread it over Owen before positioning himself over his hips. Owen grabbed onto his waist, and together they slowly eased Trevor down onto him.

"Fuck, you feel good," Owen gasped. Trevor grit his teeth as his body adjusted. Ample prep or not, Owen was a lot to take in.

His body finally relaxing, he tried one experimental roll of his hips, only to be nearly thrown off the bed when Owen bucked up.

"Sorry," Owen said sheepishly. "It's been a while. Probably won't last long."

"Same," said Trevor with a grin. He tried another roll and oh there, right there.

He let out a soft moan, and leaned forward, bracing his hands against Owen's chest. Owen gasped as Trevor ran his hands over his scars, tracing one all the way across the tight bud of a nipple.

"That hurt?"

"Naw," said Owen, running his hands up and down Trevor's sides. "Just not used to it. Only me and the doctors ever touched them before, and they certainly didn't touch them like *that*."

Trevor's heart ached for the man beneath him, and resolved to prove with his body, not just his words, how beautiful he found Owen. He continued tracing the scars as he moved over Owen, then moved on to the tattoos, treating the designs with equal reverence. The brush of his fingers along the wings of a particularly vivid bird caused Owen to buck up again before their bodies found the perfect rhythm that had them both groaning and gasping.

Trevor lay down on Owen, his entire body flush with his. The angle wasn't as good, but this way he could taste Owen, feel those plush lips against his own as his cock, slick with saliva and precome, rubbed against the flat planes of Owen's stomach.

Owen wrapped his arms around Trevor, clutching him tightly as his thrusts sped up and became more erratic.

Trevor whispered into the hollow of his throat, "That's it, Owen. So good. Come for me."

"Ah, Trev!" Owen shouted, hips driving up one last time as he climaxed. Trevor gasped as his body tightened around him. With a groan Owen thrust again. The second thrust hit Trevor just right and he cried out, shocked at the suddenness of his orgasm.

His come splashed against Owen's abs and he rolled his hips, trying to get more of Owen against him and inside him.

It seemed to go on forever, but when he finally came down, it was to the sight of Owen smiling down at where Trevor's head was pillowed on his chest. Owen ran a finger down Trevor's nose and Trevor kissed it dreamily as it passed his lips.

"You lied," Trevor said. He tapped Owen's chest with a shaky hand. "No egg beater tattoo, just a very tasteful rose. How disappointing."

He felt himself rise and fall as Owen laughed beneath him.

"You really can't shut it off, can you?" Owen grinned. "Alright, how about the rest of it? How would you rate *that*, Mr. Fancy Critic?"

"Hmm." Trevor considered, moving his hand to idly trace a pattern over Owen's shoulder once he could feel his fingers again. "Passable. Simple and without frills, but satisfactory enough, I suppose."

He grinned up at Owen. "Needs practice."

CHAPTER 16

That evening, after round two and a quick break for food—where Owen learned the truth about how favorably Trevor felt about his cooking, which led to round three before he could even suggest dessert—Owen stared at the man dozing in his arms.

They'd talked, and while Owen wasn't thrilled with Trevor's previous actions, he could understand them. Besides, round two had consisted of Trevor doing whatever he could think of to make it up to Owen. And he'd been thorough. Owen's ass twitched at the memory. Very thorough.

But now he was thinking about something he'd wanted to ask Trevor for months. Honestly, since the first time Trevor had gone over the books and pointed out where Owen was losing money. Back then, he'd known it was too hasty a decision. Now, even after all their squabbles, Owen knew it was something he had to ask. Maybe even because of their squabbles, because they came through them and ended up even stronger together.

"Hey, Trev," he said, shaking Trevor gently. "Wake up, it's important."

"Mmm, I don't think I can again," Trevor said sleepily. "But you go right ahead, I'm here for you."

Owen snorted. "Not that. Even more important."

Trevor propped his head up on Owen's chest and raised an

eyebrow at him. Owen laughed, the movement jostling Trevor up and down. He crossed his arms over Trevor's waist to keep him in place.

"I was thinking," he said slowly. He needed to make sure to use the right words for something as big as this. "We're good together."

"I agree." Trevor said with a suggestive roll of his hips.

Owen swatted the top of his ass. "Not just in bed," he continued. "You figured out all those ways to make the bakery better, and pushed me when otherwise I would've been making the same recipes until I died. And now you have someone you can tell about your work and everything without worrying about them revealing your secret. Plus, I keep you fed."

"I love you for more than just your food, Owen."

Owen relaxed at his words. Why was he so worried? This was Trev.

"Thanks," he said gruffly. "So, I was wondering. The critic thing doesn't take up all your time, right? So maybe you could come work with me? I mean, I'd feel weird paying you because of the sex, but—"

"Owen O'Neill, are you suggesting that I prostitute myself for pastries? Because I hate to break it to you: they're good, but they're not that good.

"Trev..."

"Fine, fine. You're right, they are that good. Just leave a stack of danishes on the dresser when you go."

"I was asking if you wanted to be my partner." Owen huffed. This man could exasperate a saint.

Trevor stilled in his arms. "Come again?"

"My partner. We run the business together. I do the baking; you do the books. What you said before to Yvonne? You were right. It's terrible business sense to base store hours around a single person. As much as I haven't wanted to admit it the last few months, I do have to sleep sometime. And with the new kids and everything, it's more complicated than it was before, but I think you'll like that. I've got some other ideas to run by you too."

He hesitated, unable to read the look on Trevor's face. "You don't have to. I mean, it was just a thought. We can still keep doing this if you want, without doing that. Or... neither, if you didn't want to?"

"Are you just asking me this because I'm amazing in bed and it suddenly seems like a great idea?"

Owen snorted. "No, I wanted to ask you long before I knew you were amazing in bed."

"As long as you admit it." Trevor cocked his head and looked at Owen with that piercing gaze that Owen had hated and loved since the first moment the infuriating man had walked into his bakery.

Finally, Trevor said, "Okay."

"Yeah?"

"Yeah," said Trevor, settling down again against Owen's chest. He grinned up at him. "Seal it with a kiss?"

※ ※ ※

...obviously the several-hour wait times speak for themselves. For those who arrive too late to get a "critter" or have the misfortune to be there on a day that the ever mercurial, ever astounding, Chef O'Neill decides not to make them, never fear. The new offerings at Nana O'Neill's are even better than those of my first two reviews, with the pioneering chef providing modern twists

on traditional classics that are fresh and innovative while still maintaining the phenomenally rich flavors and high standards of his original pastries.

Finally, on a personal note, I must inform my devoted readers that I will no longer be reviewing bakeries, patisseries, or—God forbid—cupcakeries. However, I will continue to review traditional restaurants with the same acerbic eye and discerning palate you have come to expect.

This follows a recent move in my personal life that would constitute a conflict of interest.

EPILOGUE

Owen was pulled out of sleep by the sound of their condo door creaking open and Trevor cursing.

"Time izzit?" he muttered when the sound of Trevor's footsteps made it to the bedroom.

"About eleven. Go back to sleep."

"M'awake now." Owen rolled over and fumbled for the bedside lamp. He finally clicked it on and rubbed his eyes as they adjusted to the sudden light. His eyes focused just in time to see Trevor drop his cufflinks in the bowl on the dresser and start unbuttoning his shirt. Mmm, definitely a view worth waking up for. Owen settled back against the pillows, hands behind his head, to watch the show.

"No really, go back to sleep. I know what an ogre you are when you don't get your beauty rest."

"I'll show you ogre," Owen muttered, before cracking his jaw with a wide yawn. "Besides, I can sleep in tomorrow. Connor and Tara are coming in for prep, and Dev said he could handle anything else that came up. So I only need to get there to make sure everything goes in the ovens when it's supposed to."

"I scheduled Connor and Tara together?" asked Trevor as he slid the shirt off his shoulders. "What was I thinking?"

"God knows. I think it was something about me working too much and them being the least likely to burn the place down if left unattended. Which is still hilarious coming from you," Owen said. "Where were you, anyhow?"

"Antoine's," Trevor reached into the closet for a hanger.

"Ohh, Antoine's. I see." In the dresser mirror, Owen caught the reflection of Trevor struggling to keep a straight face. "What's this Antoine got that I haven't?"

"Duck confit, for one." Trevor replied, as he slid his belt off and hung it on one of the many closet hooks Owen had installed for just that purpose.

"And you didn't miss anything," Trevor continued as he unbuttoned his slacks. "It was over-seasoned and over-cooked. And that was only the start of it. You know how steak tartare is meant to be raw? Well, you wouldn't believe…"

Trevor trailed off as his eyes lit up with a fire Owen knew meant that he was already thinking up devastating bon mots to completely eviscerate the restaurant in his next review. His fingers twitched like they were already flying over the keys, the gold band on his left ring finger catching the light.

Owen sighed. When Trevor told him that he was only going to be a restaurant critic part-time so he could devote even more time to helping out at Nana O'Neill's, Owen had been thrilled. He should've known better.

It turned out Trevor's definition of "part-time" was "continue shredding exactly as many overpriced restaurants in Grand River as before, only now as a freelancer making twice as much money" and "helping out" meant "while at the same time singlehandedly making Owen the most sought-after pastry chef in the state, mostly by turning important people down until they begged him to cater their events and threw stupid amounts of money at him for the privilege." Owen had suspicions Trevor had even more planned, if the way he muttered things in his sleep like "franchises… cookbook… suck it, Ramsay..." was anything to go by.

Owen hummed. But that was a worry for another day. If he wanted any chance of getting his husband into bed tonight, rather than finding him sacked out over his laptop tomorrow morning, desperate measures were called for.

"Trev," said Owen in a deep rumble that had Trevor's hands instantly stilling and his eyes locking onto Owen's. "If I knew that was what you needed, I'd have given you a good hard *duck* myself."

Trevor's jaw dropped open as he stared at Owen. His mouth worked silently for a few moments, trying to find words and failing. Owen preened even as he bit his lip to keep from laughing. It wasn't every day he stunned his husband speechless. At least not with his words.

"Oh my God, that was... that was..." Trevor stuttered. "That was *awful!*"

"Wanna show me something better?"

Trevor laughed as he slid his pants and underwear off before tossing the underwear toward the laundry hamper and turning around to hang the pants in the closet.

Nice view, *very* nice view, but still not exactly what Owen had been hoping for. He tried again.

"You know, people warned me marriage would be like this." Owen let out a sigh almost as dramatic as one of Trevor's own. "Once the honeymoon is over and you're settled into your nice, quiet home that doesn't smell like butter and burnt sugar all the time, you let the *spice* go out of the relationship. Next thing you know, your husband is out at all hours, getting it *raw* from some strange Frenchman."

"Stop, stop." Trevor laughed as crawled up the bed. He stopped when he was straddling Owen's lap, still chuckling, with one hand either side of Owen's head. Owen grinned up at him, pleased as punch. Trevor smiled back, fondness tugging at the corners of his eyes. Then Owen let out a squawk as Trevor yanked the pillow out from under his head and hit him with it.

Owen made a grab for Trevor's ticklish sides, earning him a squawk of his own, and then it was on. The ensuing wrestling match lasted several minutes, and ended with both the pillows and alarm clock being knocked to the floor and Owen pinning Trevor underneath him at the foot of the bed. Trevor squirmed, unwilling as ever to accept defeat, and Owen hissed as the full length of Trevor's naked and now sweaty body slid against his own.

"Mmm, that's how it is, huh?" he asked, leaning down to playfully nip Trevor's ear. Trevor threw his head back with a gasp and Owen added a few light bites to the side of his jaw for good measure. "You go out and eat at whoever's offering, because you don't think you can get better at home? Such a foodslut, Trev."

"Oh my God, Owen. I'm a restaurant critic, it's my job!" Trevor worked a hand free from Owen's grasp and reached up to pull Owen's head closer. Owen rewarded him with a scrape of teeth across his collarbone.

"Yeah, it's your job. So, I guess that makes you a food*whore* then. Put anything in your mouth for the right amount of pay, won't you?" Owen punctuated each word with a bite, working his way up Trevor's throat. "Dirty. Little. Foodwhore."

Trevor let out a breathless laugh, then groaned into his mouth as Owen kissed him deeply. When they finally broke apart for air, Trevor's arm slid off Owen's shoulder as he fell back, panting.

"Hey, Owen?"

"Yeah, Trev?"

"Is this talk turning you on too?"

Owen raised an eyebrow, then rolled his hips, rubbing his hard cock firmly against Trevor's own.

"Oh good," Trevor gasped. "I'd hate to think it was just me."

"God no," said Owen, diving in for another kiss. He paused, his lips a hair away from Trevor's. "This better not be a lead up to any sort of food-related dirty talk about my dick."

"Of course not," said Trevor, his eyes sliding away like the liar that he was.

"I mean it Trevor, one word about big sausages or bananas or cucumbers and you're sleeping on the couch."

"But Owen," said Trevor, blinking up at him guilelessly, "what if I want a taste of your cream?"

❋ ❋ ❋

"Here," said Yvonne at Nana O'Neill's the next day as Trevor tried to surreptitiously rub the kinks out of his neck. They needed to get a bigger couch.

She set a plate down next to his notebook on the small table. "Owen said to give you this to tide you over until his break, and I really, *really* don't want to know what that means."

She strode off before Trevor could say anything. He looked down. On the plate was a single, *massive* éclair.

Trevor looked over at the far end of the counter where Owen was kneading dough to the delight of an unnoticed but very appreciative cluster of tittering yoga moms. Owen snickered, grinning at Trevor with a quirk of a "butter wouldn't melt" smile. A smile that slowly slid off his face as Trevor wiped up a dollop of pastry cream with one finger, then without breaking eye contact, stuck out his tongue and leisurely, methodically licked it off. He then picked up the éclair in both hands and brought it up to his lips. He opened his mouth extra wide, but pulled the éclair back at the last moment.

"It's a little smaller than I'm used to!" he called out.

Owen flushed bright red and whipped his head back around to the dough. He stared down at it like he'd forgotten what it was.

Trevor smirked. Setting the éclair down, he picked up his pencil again, and ran the eraser against his bottom lip. Owen abruptly had something very important to do in the kitchen.

Trevor laughed as he stood up slowly and sauntered back to join his husband. Oh, yeah. This was going to be *sweet*.

❋ ❋ ❋

The End

BY SAMANTHA SORELLE

His Lordship's Mysteries:

His Lordship's Secret
His Lordship's Master
His Lordship's Return
Lord Alfie of the Mud (Short Story)
His Lordship's Gift (Short Story)

Other Works:

Cairo Malachi and the Adventure of the Silver Whistle
Suspiciously Sweet
The Pantomime Prince (Short Story)

HIS LORDSHIP'S SECRET

Book One Of His Lordship's Mysteries

London 1818

Alfred Pennington, the Earl of Crawford, knows someone wants him dead. An illicit boxing match seems the perfect opportunity to hire a champion fighter to watch his back, but Alfie is shocked to recognize the beaten and bloody challenger as his childhood friend, Dominick, one of the few people who knows the truth about Alfie's past.

Life has been hard for Dominick, so he can't believe his luck when Alfie—now with fine manners and a fancy title—offers him a chance to escape the slums in order to catch a potential killer. That's difficult enough, but not falling in love with the refined, confident man his friend has become may prove trickier still.

The investigation draws the two men closer than ever, but it becomes clear that their years apart may prove too much to overcome. As the danger mounts, can they find their way through the past to a future together? Or will hidden secrets cost them their happiness... and their lives?

Available Now

ABOUT THE AUTHOR

Samantha SoRelle

Sam grew up all over the world and finally settled in Southern California when she soaked up too much sunshine and got too lazy to move.

When she's not writing, she's doing everything possible to keep from writing. This has led to some unusual pastimes including but not limited to: perfecting fake blood recipes, designing her own cross-stitch patterns, and wrapping presents for tigers.

She also enjoys collecting paintings of tall ships and has lost count of the number of succulents she owns.

She can be found online at www.samanthasorelle.com, which has the latest information on upcoming projects, free reads, the mailing list, and all her social media accounts. She can also be contacted by email at samanthasorelle@gmail.com, which she is much better about checking than social media!

Made in the USA
Columbia, SC
12 February 2023